THE MOUNTAIN TAVERN

THE MOUNTAIN TAVERN
and Other Stories

BY

LIAM O'FLAHERTY

Short Story Index Reprint Series

BOOKS FOR LIBRARIES PRESS
FREEPORT, NEW YORK

PR6029
F5 M6

INTERNATIONAL STANDARD BOOK NUMBER:
0-8369-4054-7

LIBRARY OF CONGRESS CATALOG CARD NUMBER:
73-178453

PRINTED IN THE UNITED STATES OF AMERICA
BY
NEW WORLD BOOK MANUFACTURING CO., INC.
HALLANDALE, FLORIDA 33009

CONTENTS

THE MOUNTAIN TAVERN

THE PAINTED WOMAN

ONE lone star was following a little half-grown moon across an open space in the dark sky. All round, the firmament was full of sagging clouds. Some were black with hanging tails of rain that fell in far-off lands. Others were pale with the light of waning day. The stark earth was swept by a bitter wind. The dying light of the hidden sun lay brown upon its back, like the shroud upon a corpse.

Yet birds were singing in the wintry dusk. They smelt some tender current in the bitter air, telling them that spring was coming with sunlight and with flowers; as if a strange spirit passed upon the wind over the bleak rocks and the naked fields, whispering:

'Soon. Soon now. Lambs are kicking in the womb.'

Already people were preparing the ground for the sowing of their crops. Since an hour before dawn, Martin Bruty and his brother Patrick had been carrying seaweed on their mare to a field where they were going to plant potatoes. Now they were coming home, exhausted and drenched to the skin by the showers of hail that had fallen. Their hands were numb. Their sodden clothes were stained with the congealed slime of the weeds.

9

The mare walked quickly, with her neck stretched forward, shivering. Her hair was as smooth as a seal's fur. She was straddled. A long piece of canvas stuffed with straw lay on her back from tail to mane, with a basket hung on either side from two pegs in a wooden yoke. Wisps of straw from the straddle's packing trailed under her belly.

Martin Bruty sat sideways on her haunches, reclining on the canvas as on a couch, his left forearm encircling the wooden yoke. He was forty years old, tall, lean, ungainly, with big muscular limbs and a beautiful face. His eyes were soft and wistful like those of a child. His countenance was pure, like that of a young virgin. His hair was grey at the temples. He looked at the sky, at the dim, stark land, at the horse and at passing birds with wonder and awe. Whenever a bird sang, he looked towards the spot whence the sweet sound came and his lips parted. He looked simple, kind, gentle, without care.

Patrick walked behind the mare, stepping very quickly in order to keep pace with her. He was five years older than his brother, yet he looked much younger. He was small and stout, with very short legs. He walked nervously, taking tiny steps and looking in all directions without noticing anything. He frowned and sniffed. There was a greedy look in his little blue eyes. His large white eyebrows moved up and down and he twitched his forehead when he sniffed. His cheeks were as red as beet-roots. His cap was stuck at the back of his round skull, showing a bald patch over his forehead. He looked restless, unhappy, unpleasant, completely out of harmony with nature that was whispering of spring, young buds, sunshine and happiness.

He carried two pitchforks on his left shoulder. In his right hand he had a can of milk. They walked in silence. The canvas of the straddle creaked against its wooden yoke. The horse's hoofs rang against the loose stones of the road. The wind whistled. The sea moaned in the distance. There were sounds of other horses, afar off, coming home and of people calling, in the village, at the top of the winding road that was bound by grey stone fences, ascending. The village was dimly visible at the summit of the hill, on the border of a wide barren crag. People were lighting their lamps and fowls were cackling as they waddled home from the pond.

Near the village, they overtook a woman who was walking with a little boy. She answered their saluta-tion in a gay voice. They passed on. When they had rounded a corner, Patrick leaned against the fence and said to his brother:

'I'll be up after you. Bring the horse to the field.

I'll light the fire and have tea ready when you come back.'

'All right,' said Martin, without looking at his brother.

He rode on. After a few yards, he suddenly sat erect, struck the horse in the flank with his foot and urged her on with an oath. She broke into a quick trot. His face darkened. He rode into the village at a gallop.

Huddled together, surrounded by stone fences, the houses were coloured like the savage wilderness about them, grey and bleak. In the dusk, their thatch and their whitewashed walls, drenched with rain that dripped from their eaves, looked as grey and desolate as the stones. The wind howled among them, sweeping across the naked crags from the cliffs beyond. To left and right, the rocky land rose in terraces to the black horizons. There was a smell of peat on the wind, acrid, making the scene still more melancholy.

Yet there was peace there and birds sang upon the gables of the houses, singing of golden, mellow summer dusks.

He rode the mare, through a gap in the fence, into the yard of a house in the centre of the village. The mare halted at the closed door of a barn on the left side of the yard. She shuddered and began to munch at wisps of straw that lay on the ground. Martin dismounted, opened the barn door, brought out a dish of raw potatoes and gave them to her. She whinnied and began to gobble them up, gripping them with difficulty between her soft, thick lips. He uncovered her. She spread out her four legs, shook herself and cleared her nostrils with a loud noise. Then he rubbed her from head to foot with a bunch of straw. Where the straddle had lain, her hide was hot and moist with perspiration. There was a big bay patch there. The rest of her hide was dark with rain. Everywhere he touched her hide, rubbing her, the hide trembled violently.

Now and again, while he worked, he glanced over his shoulder down the road. Each time his face darkened and he muttered an oath. Then again, as he turned to the mare, his face grew tender and he spoke to her as he rubbed her.

He bound up the straddle with a rope, hung the baskets on pegs in the barn wall, put the straddle into the barn, closed the door, mounted the mare and rode away. Now the mare snorted, straining at the halter, trying to break into a gallop. He brought her to a field among the hills, a mile from the house. It was pitch-dark when he returned.

There was a light in the house. Smoke rose from the chimney. Smoke also issued in gusts through the door, buffeted by a contrary wind. The house looked dreary. There were no curtains on the windows. The yard was wild, muddy, overgrown with weeds. The walls were almost black for want of whitewash.

When Martin entered, Patrick was on his knees on the hearth, blowing at a newly-made peat fire, over which a kettle was hanging from an iron hook. Little red flames ran to and fro among the sods of peat when he blew. When his breath died away, the flames vanished and a cloud of smoke arose from the fire. He did not look up when Martin entered.

'This fire is enough to break the heart in a stone,' he said. 'The rain must have come in on it in the barn. Strain the milk.'

'Isn't the kettle boiled yet, then?' said Martin. 'Is it only now you're lighting the fire?'

'How could I have it lit?' said Patrick angrily, without looking up. 'I'm only just after coming in.'

'What kept you then?'

'I had business.'

'Blood an' ouns.'

Martin strode to the dresser and seized the can of milk violently. His eyes were flashing.

'You had business,' he muttered. 'A fine business you had. The parish is talking about you.'

Patrick went on blowing the fire.

'Throw a little paraffin on that,' said Martin, as he poured the milk through a cloth into another can.

'No,' said Patrick, jumping to his feet. 'I'll go out to the barn and chip a few slices of that plank we got from the wreck last year. It's no use wasting paraffin.'

Martin looked after him angrily as he went out. He muttered to himself:

'We could buy a lot of paraffin with all the money he spends on drink and chasing after every strip of a woman in the parish.'

When Patrick returned with the chips, he said:

'This is no life, returning hungry to an empty house.'

'I've heard you say that often enough,' said Martin. 'We weren't put on this earth to enjoy ourselves, but to save our souls.'

'Ach!' said Patrick sourly, as he stooped over the fire with the chips. 'A man would be better dead than listening to your grumbling.'

'Who is doing the grumbling?' said Martin.

'That's enough of it,' said Patrick. 'That's enough now. Be putting the things on the table.'

'I'll take off my wet things first,' said Martin. ''Twill be years before that kettle boils.'

He began to strip off his clothes.

The fire blazed up, making a brighter light than

the tin paraffin lamp that hung on a nail in the wall. The delft on the dresser shone. Now there was no smoke. Patrick shut the door. Then he too began to strip.

'These three years since mother died,' he said, 'are worse than all the hardship I ever had in my life. A house without a woman is worse than hell.'

' Say Lord have mercy on her, when you speak of her,' said Martin.

'Every damn thing I say, you pick me up,' shouted Patrick. 'What have you against me? Eh?'

Naked, Martin walked to the hearth and took dry clothes from a line that stretched across the chimney.

'Mind that kettle,' he said. 'It's going to boil.'

They both dressed in dry clothes and hung their wet ones on the line. They laid the table for a meal of tea and bread and butter. Patrick made tea. They sat down to eat. The table was without a cloth. The cups had no saucers. The loaf lay on the naked board. The butter was also lying on the board, with a bedraggled thin paper about it. The milk lay in the three-quart can into which it had been strained.

They ate hurriedly, in silence. Then Patrick went to the hearth to refill his cup from the teapot. At the fire he said:

'I'm not going to stick this any longer. One of us has to stir.'

'Pour some into this,' said Martin, reaching over his cup.

Patrick returned to the table and continued to eat. He kept glancing at his brother furtively, his white eyebrows moving up and down.

'What did you say ?' he muttered after some time.

'Me?' said Martin. 'I said nothing.'

'Didn't you hear what I said?'

'What did you say?'

'I said it was time for one of us to get married.'

Martin pushed away his empty cup, put the can of milk to his head and drank a large quantity of the milk. He wiped his mouth, crossed himself and went to the fire.

'You have something on your mind,' he said. 'Out with it.'

He took a piece of tobacco from his waistcoat pocket and bit it. Patrick also drank some of the milk, crossed himself, put on his cap and came to the fire. He lit his pipe with a coal. They both sat in silence, on stools, one smoking his pipe, the other chewing.

'Well!' said Martin at length, spitting into the fire. 'Out with it.'

'Well!' said Patrick. 'I have this on my mind. It's time for one of us to bring in a woman here. A man would be better dead than living this way.

There's nobody to clean or wash or get a meal ready for us after the day's work. We haven't had a pig this last year. There's money lost. Potatoes are going to rot in the barn. I'd rather let them rot than sell them for the few shillings they give for them in the shops. We could feed ten pigs in the year. Sheep too. We can't keep a sheep because we have no time to run after them over the rocks. We're losing money, along with the loneliness and misery of an empty house.'

'Money!' said Martin. 'You can't bring it to the grave with you. Haven't we enough to eat? But you may do as you please. You've been driving at this a long time and I'd rather have anything than hearing all the tongues in the parish jeering at our name on account of your blackguarding.'

'What blackguarding?' said Patrick angrily.

'You and Kate Tully,' said Martin in a loud voice. 'You follow her wherever she goes.'

'Well!' said Patrick. 'I'll follow her no longer. And less of your tongue, I'm telling you. You don't know what you're saying.'

'How?'

'How? This is how. I asked her coming up the road and she agreed.'

Martin spat his chew into the fire, looked at his brother with open mouth and then said:

'Tare an' ouns! You asked Kate Tully to marry you?'

'I did. What about it?'

Martin's face suddenly lost its angry look. His eyes became sad and weary. His jaw dropped.

'Eh?' said Patrick. 'What's the matter? Were ye . . . were ye thinking of asking her yerself?'

'Me?' said Martin, flushing and raising his head. 'I'd rather lie with a dog than with the woman,' he added fiercely.

'Be careful of what you are saying,' said Patrick in a low voice.

'I'll say what's in my mind,' said Martin. 'Now is the time to say it, isn't it? She's been fifteen years in America without tale or tidings of her. Then she returned last year with a boy and no husband.'

'Her husband is dead,' said Patrick angrily. 'What are you driving at?'

'Maybe he is,' said Martin. 'A woman doesn't go about here with a painted face, though, if she is right. What for does she paint her face and lips and terrify every decent man with her language and her free ways, unless . . .'

'Unless what?'

Martin shuddered and became silent. Patrick was watching him with glittering eyes.

'God knows,' said Martin sadly, 'it's hard to

think badly of her, after what she was before she
went away. Ye'd stand in the snow looking at her
lovely face and she was so shy and modest that she
blushed when a man bid her the time of day. Now
she is. . . . Ach!'

'Now, listen to me here,' said Patrick. 'I've had
enough of this. Remember what I'm saying. I'm
going to marry Kate Tully. If you don't like it,
there's the door. You can take your share of the
land and money and get a wife for yourself.'

'You're not marrying her,' said Martin. 'You're
marrying her fortune of three hundred pounds.'

'Well, there you are now,' said Patrick. 'Think
over it. I'll have no argument. I've wasted the best
of my life, each of us watching the other. You
always had a sour mouth whenever I thought of a
woman. But I'll wait no longer.'

'Marry her then,' said Martin, jumping to his
feet. 'Marry her. But I'll stay here. This is my
father's house. You can't put me out of it. Marry
her and the devil take you and her.'

He strode to the door. Patrick jumped up and
shouted:

'Where are you going? Take back what you said.'

Martin turned back and looked at his brother
gloomily. Then he shuddered, bent his head and
murmured sadly:

'I'm sorry, Paddy. I . . . I . . . To-morrow we can . . . I'll go out for a bit.'

He went out. Patrick sat down again by the fire and smoked. His face twitched. Then he also jumped to his feet and left the house. He visited his uncle. He returned at midnight and went to bed. Martin had not yet returned. At two o'clock in the morning he was awakened by hearing Martin come into the room.

'Where were you till this hour?' he said.

'I was over to the cliffs to see was there any wreckage,' said Martin.

'How could you see in the dark, man alive?'

'Never mind,' said Martin. 'I was listening to the sound of the sea.'

'Ugh!' said Patrick, turning towards the wall. 'You're out of your head.'

'Maybe I am,' said Martin.

He got into bed beside his brother, but he lay awake all night, thinking.

Next day, while they were at the seashore loading seaweed on the mare, Martin said to his brother:

'Have you still got a mind to do what you were talking of last night?'

'I have,' said Patrick.

Martin brought the loaded mare to the field, dropped the load and returned. Then he said:

'Very well. We better go home at noon and dress ourselves. A settlement has to be made.'

'We'll do that,' said Patrick, 'in the name of God.'

'I hope God will bless it,' said Martin gloomily.

In the afternoon, Patrick went on the mare to the town and returned with a bottle of whisky. After dark, they went with their uncle and another man to the house where Kate Tully lived with her married brother. They made the match. Martin agreed to everything they said. He appeared to be quite satisfied. It was decided to have the marriage in a week's time. Next day they went to the parish priest to sign the agreement.

There were thirty acres of land, a horse, a cow, a bullock, a yearling calf, the house and furniture and a boat. Martin gave his share of all this property to his brother, excepting his share of the boat. The boat was to be owned in common by the two of them. In return, Patrick gave Martin his share of their common savings, which amounted to four hundred pounds. It was arranged that Martin should go on living in the house until he married. He was to receive one-fifth of the house's earnings, in return for his work.

The priest tried to point out to them that this arrangement might cause some difficulty later on and that it was better that Martin should at once set about making a home of his own, but Martin refused to hear of it. He said he was now too old to marry.

Kate Tully also had a clause inserted in the agreement to the effect that, in case of her death, her son Charles should inherit the property equally with any children she might have by Patrick. Patrick agreed to this after some argument.

After they had signed the agreement, they went to celebrate in the town, but Martin refused to accompany them. Neither did he give any assistance in the preparation for the wedding. He went about his ordinary work.

Patrick, on the other hand, went about in his best clothes, talking loudly, drinking, superintending the preparations, treating all his friends with the extravagance of a mean man carried away by a sudden passion. He hardly slept at all.

'Why don't you drink with me?' he said to Martin. 'Why are you gloomy? Have you anything against me?'

'This is not a time for drinking and merrymaking,' said Martin. 'It's your prayers you should be saying approaching a sacrament, instead of leering at the thought of your marriage bed.'

'Pruth!' said Patrick. 'Bloody woes! What a monk you are!'

Martin heard the people whispering and mocking

at his brother, because he was going to marry a withered woman, who already had a child. Children, as is the custom when there is a marriage in a house, used to call after him, shouting: 'Kate Tully.' Instead of paying no attention to this harmless teasing, he was deeply mortified.

Patrick spent money freely on the preparations. His uncle's wife and two other women were brought in. They scoured out the house, whitewashed it, put curtains on the windows, delft on the dresser, new sheets on the beds. Whisky, porter, wine and a large quantity of food was purchased. A sack of flour was baked into bread.

The whole countryside came to the wedding. The kitchen and the two bedrooms were packed with people. Only a few had room to sit in the kitchen. The rest stood, row behind row, around the little space in the centre where couples were dancing. A man sat on a chair near the fire playing an accordion. Three men went round serving whisky and porter. Out in the yard there was a group of young men, drinking heavily, boasting and discussing feats of strength. In the bigger bedroom, where the marriage bed was prepared, people were eating in relays. Women passed back and forth, carrying teapots from the kitchen fire. Other women hustled guests to the table. Patrick went around shouting, already quite

24

drunk, urging everybody to be merry. There was an air of reckless savagery and haste about the whole thing, and the older people noticed a lack of decency and of respect. They were whispering to one another.

Martin, sitting gloomily in a corner of the hearth, noticed that people had no respect for the house or for the marriage. He heard the whispering. He felt terribly ashamed and angry. He thought it was about him they were whispering, that they were jeering at him. So he refused to eat or drink. He sat without movement, with his eyes on the fire. He wanted to get up, leave the house and stand on the cliffs, looking out at the sea; but he would not move, lest they might jeer still more at him for running away. And yet it was a torture to stay. He was aware of the little boy, Kate's son, who was sitting in the opposite corner of the hearth. He was aware of Kate herself, who sat in triumph near the musician. He hated them all. Henceforth they would all be in the house with him. He would stand naked before the people, a butt for people's scorn. So he thought.

Every time Kate spoke in her loud, gay, rasping voice, he shuddered. And yet he could hardly restrain himself from looking at her.

Everybody was watching her and she seemed partly to enjoy the attention she attracted and partly to resent it. She sat with her legs crossed. Her dress was so short that a red garter showed on her thigh above the knee. She kept tapping her foot on the floor and pulling down her skirt that refused to go any farther than the brink of her knee. Her legs were beautiful. She wore silk stockings. Her dress was gaudy. It was red. Her cheeks and lips were painted. She was very slim and she had an exquisite figure. But her broad shoulders were bony. Her chest was flat. Her hair was dyed a yellowish colour. Her face bore the remains of great beauty. But her eyes were hard and her mouth was coarse. Although she was only thirty-five years of age she looked old. All that was left of her youthful beauty was a skeleton. She had, however, that power of attraction which comes of knowledge. The coolness of her manner, the cynical, brusque way in which she spoke, the glitter in her strange eyes were more exciting than the freshness of young beauty. She kept smiling. Her smile was contemptuous. With her mouth she enjoyed her triumph. But her eyes sometimes had a look of fear in them.

Her son was even more strange than she. He was six years old, pale, delicate and shy. He looked alien. His skin was yellow. His ears were large and strangely fashioned. His neck was long and thin. He had hardly any chin. His wrists were like spindles. His thin legs bent inwards at the knees. His upper teeth protruded. He kept eating sweets from a paper bag and looking casually at the dancers, without any excitement.

Patrick kept going up to his wife and putting his arm around her and saying:

'I have you now.'

Then he got so drunk that they put him lying on the marriage bed in the big bedroom. Then Kate danced with the young men and drank punch in the little bedroom with the women.

When it was nearly dawn, Patrick awoke from his drunken sleep, drank some whisky and came into the kitchen. He went up to his wife and began to caress her passionately in front of the people, mumbling:

'I have you now.'

The guests began to leave. Martin heard them laugh as they went away, shouting: 'I have you now.'

Before they had all left the house, Patrick dragged his wife into the bedroom and locked the door. The little boy lay asleep in the corner of the hearth, forgotten. The uncle was the last to leave. He said to Martin:

'Where is little Charley going to sleep?'

'His bed is in his mother's room,' said Martin.

The uncle tittered drunkenly and said:

'You had better take him into your bed to-night, Martin, in the little room. It's not right to disturb a couple on their marriage night.'

Then the uncle went away. It was daylight. Martin took the little fellow in his arms and carried him into the little bedroom. The boy woke up and started on finding himself in a stranger's arms. He began to call for his mother. He struck at Martin's chest with his little fists. Martin put him into his own bed without undressing him. Then he lay on the bed, soothing the child. The child fell asleep.

Then Martin went into the kitchen and sat by the fire. He heard Patrick snoring. He jumped to his feet and dashed out of the house, leaving the door open. He went up to the cliffs and wandered around there. He came back to the house, took the can and milked the cow. When he returned with the milk, Kate had arisen. She was busy tidying the house and getting breakfast ready.

'Hello!' she said gaily. 'You didn't go to bed?'

She was full of energy and yet she looked horrible, like an old woman. There was no paint on her face. Her cheeks were hollow. Her lips were cracked and yellow like those of a corpse. She was wearing a loose wrap, belted at the waist. She wore slippers without heels on her bare feet. Her hair was bedraggled, streaming around her neck. He looked at

28

her in amazement and said nothing. Then he sat in the corner of the hearth, waiting for his breakfast.

She took no notice of him. She hummed a tune as she worked and she worked at great speed, deftly. She gave him his breakfast and brought tea into bed to her husband. Martin heard his brother growl when she wakened him. Then his brother called out:

'Martin.'

'What?'

'Start cutting potato seeds. We'll begin sowing to-morrow.'

Martin said nothing. But he thought:

'He orders me like a servant before her.'

He became inflamed with anger. He left his breakfast and went out. He stood outside the door, trying to rebel against his brother, but it was alien to his nature. He could not do so. The child awoke and began to cry.

'What the devil is the matter with that child?' grumbled Patrick.

'I'll run in and see,' said Kate. 'He probably finds himself strange.'

Martin walked away. He entered the barn and began to cut potato seeds. Later, Patrick joined him. They worked together in silence. Neither referred to the wedding. Patrick looked cross and discontented. The child came out of the house and began to play

29

in the yard, uttering loud cries and calling his mother to look at things which he found strange.

'He won't live,' said Patrick. 'What do you think?'

Martin said nothing.

'No. He won't live,' said Patrick. 'His father was a foreigner. They have bad blood in them.'

At dinner the child was cranky and refused the food that was given him. His mother suddenly lost her temper and beat the boy. The boy went into hysterics. Patrick jumped up, cursed and left the house.

'Tare an' ouns,' Martin called after him. 'Have ye no more nature in you that to curse at a child?

'Mind your own business,' shouted Patrick from the yard.

Martin took the boy in his arms and began to soothe him.

'Don't spoil him,' said Kate. 'It's just temper.'

Martin looked at her angrily. She dropped her eyes, caught the child from his arms and began to kiss it. Then she sat down and burst into tears, rocking the child and murmuring:

'You poor little orphan. I don't know what to do with you.'

Martin went out. That evening, when the child was being put to bed, Patrick said:

'Hadn't you better put his little bed into Martin's room?'

'Why so?' said Martin.

'Nothing,' said Patrick. 'Only . . . only I thought he might keep you company. You never liked being alone at night.'

Martin looked at his brother savagely.

'Do what you like,' he said. 'You're master here.'

They put the child into Martin's room. That night, when he came in after visiting in a neighbour's house, he stood for a long time over the little bed, in the dark, listening to the child's breathing. He pitied the child and at the same time hated his brother. He realized that his brother was jealous of the child.

A few days later, while they were working in the field sowing potatoes, Patrick said:

'You're spoiling that child. You had better not be coddling him. He's nothing to us anyway. His father was a foreigner.'

'Every child was made by God,' said Martin. 'Kindness won't spoil anything.'

'It's time you were thinking of getting a wife for yourself, then,' said Patrick, 'as you're so fond of children.'

The Spring came. The dark earth became a paradise. It was good to smell the wind that was scented with the perfume of growth. Bird music was triumphant. The cold sunlight glittered on the black earth uprooted by the sowers. Each dawn was wild with the cries of living things going forth to labour. Each dusk was full of tender murmurs, as tired men happily sought their beds and cows lowed for their milkers and sheep bleated over their new-born lambs. All evil passions were silenced by man's frenzied efforts to satisfy the energy born of the earth's awakening.

Yet it was a false peace that fell upon the house. The silence grew as menacing as a dark cloud that hangs in the sky on a sultry day, foretelling thunder.

A great change came over Kate. She no longer put paint upon her cheeks and lips. She cast aside her foreign clothes and dressed in the manner of a peasant. She did the housework with enthusiasm and skill. She left nothing undone. She dropped her brusque, gay manner. She became serious. She no longer talked of anything but of the house, the crops, the cattle. She no longer looked alien. She became a peasant woman again. She grew bold in the house and spoke curtly to her husband. She put on flesh. Her eyes lost their strange, lascivious look. Instead, they became avaricious. Her cheeks, that had been hollow and yellow like the cheeks of a corpse beneath the paint, now filled out and became tanned brown by the healthy air and wind. Her lips and fingers no longer twitched nervously. She was no longer taken by hysterical bursts of passion. She became like a rock in which there is neither softness nor passion. Now she did not inspire desire. Although her attraction still remained great, she reacted differently on men. Women of the village began to speak well of her.

She treated both men with equal coldness, as if neither were her husband. And in the evening, when they had returned from work and were sitting by the fire before going to bed, she talked to her child instead of talking to them.

Neither did the child become friendly with either of them. He still remained an alien. He improved in health and became bold, playing about the house as if he had been born there; but whenever he looked at the brothers there was a vacant stare in his eyes, as if they were strangers to him. When Patrick scowled at him, he sighed and went to his mother. When Martin tried to play with him or gave him toys which he had whittled with a knife, he remained silent and as lifeless as a girl with a man whom she does not love.

Yet Martin was not offended by the boy's manner. His kindness to the boy pleased him because it irritated his brother. He was pleased also with the change that had taken place in Kate. He was pleased with her coldness towards her husband. He was pleased with the gloomy, discontented look that had settled on his brother's countenance. He had become bitter. He no longer found pleasure in the sea, nor in the singing of birds, nor in watching the starry sky at night. A mocking, malicious spirit had taken possession of his mind, driving out all other pleasures but that of making his brother unhappy.

Spring passed. Now warm breezes sang among the swaying fields of corn. People became idle watching the growth of their crops. It was good to lie in a glen in the sunlight among the wild, sweet flowers.

The brothers stayed about the house, drawn irresistibly towards the cause of the bitter enmity that was growing in their minds.

One morning, Martin was making a top for the little boy by the fire. The boy stood near, watching. Patrick sat in the corner of the hearth, smoking. Kate was out in the yard, attending to young pigs they had just bought.

Suddenly Patrick said to the child:

'Hey, Charley, did you have a top in America?'

'Yes, I had,' said the child. 'I had three.'

'Who made them for you?' said Patrick. 'Your father?'

34

'No. Mammy bought them in a shop.'

'Didn't your daddy make any tops for you?'

' No,' said the child. 'I don't remember my daddy.'

'Leave the child alone,' said Martin angrily.

Patrick's little eyes gleamed. He sniffed and moved his white eyebrows up and down.

'What was your daddy's name?' he continued.

'My daddy's name was John.'

'John what? What was his other name?'

'John Smith,' said the boy.

'Bloody woes,' said Patrick. 'That's a handy name to have. Where was he from?'

'Leave the child alone,' shouted Martin.

'What's up now?' cried Kate from the yard.

'Wasn't your daddy called Martin?' continued Patrick.

The child began to cry. He ran out into the yard to his mother. Martin jumped to his feet and cried:

'You leave that child alone. Do you hear?'

Patrick jumped up and shouted:

'Whose house is this? Clear out if you don't like it. I'll have none of your impudence.'

Kate came in, holding the boy by the hand.

'What's this?' she cried. 'What were you doing to the child?'

'I asked him a civil question about his father,'

35

shouted Patrick. 'Haven't I a right to know who the brat's father was, seeing I'm keeping him?'

Kate ran to the hearth and picked up the tongs.

'I'll brain you with this,' she hissed, 'if you say another word.'

Martin caught her.

'Don't you hit him,' he cried. 'Let me deal with him.'

'So that's it, is it?' cried Patrick. 'You've changed your mind about her since the night you said you'd rather lie with a dog than with her.'

'Liar,' shouted Martin, turning pale.

'You can have her now, then,' said Patrick. 'She's a dry bag. I've been sold a blind pup. There was nothing in her womb but that sick vermin that doesn't know his own father. My curse on the house.'

He rushed out. As he passed the child he made a kick at it. The child screamed. Kate dropped on to a chair, put her fingers between her teeth and bit them. Martin stood before the hearth, trembling. Then he cursed, took his tobacco from his pocket and bit at it. He began to chew. Kate began to tremble. Then she began to sob hysterically.

'Look here,' said Martin to her angrily. 'I did you wrong. He said the truth. I said what you heard just now. But don't you be afraid. I'll do right by you now. That savage won't raise a hand to your child while I'm here.'

He left the house.

All that day, Patrick went among the neighbours, complaining that his wife treated him with cruelty, that she was barren, that there was a scar on her stomach, that her womb had been extracted in an hospital, that she favoured his brother, that she was robbing him in the interests of her child. He returned late at night. His wife was waiting for him. She received him as if nothing had happened and gave him his supper.

Martin returned from a visit while Patrick was having his supper. He glanced with hatred at his brother and immediately went into his room.

Patrick called after him:

'We'll begin to-morrow making a field of that crag beyond the Red Meadow. There is going to be no one eating the bread of idleness in this house.'

'All right,' said Martin calmly from his room.

Then he stood near the bed of the sleeping child, listening to the child's breath, in the darkness. His face broke into a smile and his eyes glittered. When he got into bed he kept laughing to himself. He kept waking through the night and listening to the child's breathing and laughing to himself.

37

Next day they brought crowbars and a sledge and they went to the crag beyond the Red Meadow. They began to quarry the rocks. They worked savagely, excited by their hatred of one another. Patrick ordered his brother about, treating him like a servant. Martin obeyed meekly and smiled in a strange manner at his brother's oaths.

That evening, while they were having supper, he said suddenly to Kate:

'I've been thinking, this while back, that I should make a will. No man knows when his hour is going to come and it's best to put things in a way that there'll be no quarrel over my few pounds after I'm gone.'

Patrick looked up suspiciously. His little eyes flashed. His neck became florid. His white eyebrows moved up and down. Then he said:

'It's not of your death you should be thinking, but of getting a wife. If you had the guts of a man you'd look for a wife.'

Martin smiled faintly and went on talking to Kate. Kate's eyes became small. She watched Martin like a bird.

'I've been thinking,' he said, 'this while back, that little Charley has been a great comfort to me since he came into the house. I'd like to think that maybe when he grew up and I'm gone he'd have something

38

to think well of me for. So, I'm thinking of making a will.'

Then he arose from the table and went out. Kate put her apron to her eye, as if to wipe away a tear. But her eyes were dry and her face was flushed.

Patrick looked at the table with his mouth open. Then he caught up a piece of the bread that Kate had baked, crushed it between his fingers and growled:

'Do you call that bread? It's like putty. I wouldn't give it to a dog.'

He threw the bread at the child and said:

'Here. Catch that.'

Then he cursed and went out of the house. Kate showed no sign of resentment in her cold, hawk-like countenance.

Next day, while they were digging out the stones from the crag, Patrick said to his brother:

'Wake up, you fool. Don't loaf around. Is it thinking of your will you are? Did you make that will yet?'

'I'm thinking about it,' said Martin calmly. 'I want to put it in a way that nobody can touch my money but the child. I have to think about it.'

'The curse of God on you,' said Patrick with great violence.

He dropped his crowbar and left the crag. He came home and shouted at his wife:

'Give me some money.'

She gave him a pound note.

'I want more,' he said.

'That's all there is in the house,' she said quietly.

'I'll have a look then,' he said.

He rushed into the bedroom and tried to open her trunk. She ran in after him and said:

'Leave that alone.'

'What have you in it?' he cried. 'Why do you keep it locked?'

'It's none of your business,' she said. 'I gave you three hundred pounds when I came into the house. That's all you bargained for.'

'Ha!' he cried. 'You have money in it. You kept money from me. You are stealing the money of the house for your bastard child. You have taken my land. You got around my fool of a brother to leave you his money and now you –'

'Shut up,' she hissed at him, 'or I'll brain you.'

He rushed at her and felled her with a blow of his fist. Then he became terrified and fled from the house. When Martin returned from the crag, Kate was going about her work calmly. He noticed that she had a black bruise on her cheek. He asked her what had happened. She told him.

He smiled strangely and said:

'I'm going into the town.'

When he returned in the evening, he handed her a document.

'That's the will,' he said. 'In case God sends for me, Charley will have every penny I own. Look after that.'

She kissed his hand and brought the will to her trunk. Putting it in, her eyes glittered and she sat for a long time before the open trunk, sucking her lips and smiling.

Patrick returned drunk that night, but he went to bed quietly. Next day, when they were working on the crag, Martin said to him:

'I didn't see you in the town yesterday.'

Patrick looked at him and said nothing.

'I went in to make that will I was talking about,' said Martin calmly.

Patrick remained silent.

'It's all settled now,' continued Martin quietly, 'so my mind is at peace.'

'Listen,' whispered Patrick savagely.

Martin looked at him.

'Watch yourself,' whispered Patrick.

They glared at one another. Their faces were white with hatred.

'I'm satisfied,' whispered Martin through his teeth.

After that they became silent and avoided each other. Kate assumed complete charge of the house. She ordered them about.

'The horse needs water,' she would say. 'One of you go and bring her to the well.'

Again she would say:

'The cow is starving in that field. Change her, one of you, to the Red Meadow.'

She never called either of them by name, but spoke to them in common, as if they were strangers. It was she who treated with neighbours about cases of trespass and she paid the rates and the rent that came due in summer.

Neither of the brothers paid any attention to her. They watched one another ceaselessly. Their eyes became fixed.

Suddenly a wild hurricane came raging over the ocean. The sun, moon and stars were hidden day and night behind a wall of black clouds that belched rain upon the earth and clashing in their flight from the shrieking gale, set the firmament on fire and shook the cliffs with the thunderous echoes of their bursting. The sea rose to the summits of the cliffs and its foam was carried on the wind far into the land. Even the wild seagulls fled into the village and stood upon the gables of the houses and screamed in horror.

For three days the storm lasted. Then the wind died. The sun appeared. The sky grew clear. The waves began to fall, heaving like wounded animals, into the sea's back. Rafts of curdled foam and torn weeds, speckled with jetsam, floundered to the shore. People came to look for wreckage.

In the evening Patrick said to his brother:

'Be ready at dawn. We are going in the boat to look for wreckage.'

Martin answered him:

'I'm satisfied.'

They both went to bed. Neither slept. Each kept rising in the night and going to the window to see if dawn had yet broken. Kate also lay awake. A cock crew an hour before dawn. At once both brothers began to put on their clothes hurriedly. Kate also arose and threw a coat over her nightdress:

Martin was the first to get to the kitchen. He cried in a loud voice:

'Are you ready now?'

Patrick came into the kitchen, followed by Kate.

'You had better take some bread, one of you,' she said. 'You'll be hungry before you get back.'

'We won't need bread,' said Patrick. 'Get the rope, you. Where is the rope?'

'I'll get it,' said Martin, going out to the barn.

Patrick began to fumble in the pockets of his waistcoat.

'Why have you on your new waistcoat?' she said. 'You have your new cap on too.'

'Mind your business,' he said. 'Give me my old waistcoat.'

She brought it to him. He took it aside and took a knife from its pocket. He put it furtively into the pocket of the waistcoat he was wearing. She saw him, but said nothing. Her eyes became fixed.

Martin came in, carrying a coil of rope on his arm.

'Are you ready now?' he said.

Without speaking Patrick moved to the door.

'Wait,' said Kate, 'till I sprinkle the Holy Water on you.'

They both went out without answering her. She picked up a little cruet of Holy Water that hung on a nail in the wall by the window. She ran out into the yard after them and shook Holy water on each of them with her forefinger. Neither of them blessed himself.

Then she returned to the house, went into the child's room and stood by his little bed, watching him and listening to his breathing.

The brothers walked in silence through the village and along the rocky road over the crags to the shore. Their boat lay bottom upwards within a fence of stones above the mound of boulders that lined the shore. They knocked down the fence at the prow and at the stern. Then they raised the prow. Martin crawled under the boat, raised it higher and rested his shoulders against the front seat. Patrick crawled in astern, put his shoulders against the third seat and straightened himself.

'Go ahead,' he said.

They moved off, carrying the boat on their shoulders. Its black, canvas-covered hulk, with their legs sticking from beneath, moving slowly over the rocks, made it look like a beetle. They brought it to the brink of the tide and stepping into the water, they laid it, mouth upwards, with a splashing sound, upon the waves. Patrick held it to the shore while Martin brought the oars and the rope. They put the oars on the thole-pins and threw the rope into the stern.

'Keep your hand on her,' said Patrick, about to step aboard.

'You hold her,' said Martin. 'I'm going in the prow same as I always do.'

'No,' said Patrick in a whisper. 'I'm going in the prow to-day.'

They looked at one another coldly. Their eyes were fixed.

'Go ahead,' said Martin. 'It's all the same to me.'

45

'Why so?' said Patrick through his teeth.

'Go ahead,' said Martin, 'seeing you want to go in the prow.'

'It's all the same to me too,' said Patrick softly. 'I'll go in the stern, same as I always do.'

'You'll go where you said you'd go,' said Martin, 'or I'll stay on the rock.'

They glared at one another again. Then Patrick stepped into the boat, sat on the front seat and seized the oars. Martin pushed off the boat and jumped aboard. They began to row eastwards towards the cliffs.

The sea was still disturbed. Although its dark surface was unbroken, there were deep hollows between the waves that came rolling quickly to the shore. The light coracle bounded from wave to wave, bobbing like a little bird in flight against the wind.

The sun began to rise as they turned a promontory. The sea glittered. They rowed close to the cliffs that rose above them precipitously. There was a loud sound of birds coming forth to fish from their caverns. Seagulls soared about them. The sea was littered with refuse. Now and again, the fin of a shark cut the surface. Gannets swooped from on high and fell like bullets, with a thud, into the floating rafts of weeds.

Masses of weeds, shining in the sunlight, lay among the broken rocks at the base of the cliffs.

They rowed quickly, searching the sea and the shore for wreckage. They had rowed three miles when at last they saw a great beam floating near the shore in a raft of weeds.

'There's a beam,' said Patrick. 'Put a noose on the rope.'

Martin shipped his oars and made a noose with the end of the rope. He tied the other end to the central seat. They rowed towards the beam. The beam rushed back and forth, on the ebbing tide. There was a heavy swell. The great piece of timber sometimes raised its head aloft from the mass of floating weeds, like a great sea monster nosing at the air. They rowed around it, seeking a chance to encircle its snout with the noose as it rose upon a wave.

Martin hurled the noose three times without success. Then at last the beam came rushing at them, carried on a great receding wave and as Patrick wheeled the boat to avoid its crashing into them, it passed close to their quarter, with its barnacled snout raised up. Martin threw the noose. It caught. Patrick groaned and lay on his oars. The rope went taut. The boat shivered. The beam swung round, held by the taught noose and turned its snout to the boat's stern. Martin caught his oars and began to row. They turned towards home, followed by the wallowing beam.

Its great weight swung the boat from side to side when the heavy swell came against it. Again it came rushing with upraised snout at the boat when the swell came with it. Rowing with all their force, they had to tack to and fro to avoid its crashing into them. The rope, tied to the vacant seat amidships, passed under Martin's seat, and ran through a notch in the stern to the log, rasping against the wood. Now it lay buried in the water, slack, as the log was hurtled towards them by the sea. Now it hung taut above the waves, dripping with brine.

Now there were many fins of sharks following the boat, keeping pace. Overhead, seagulls soared on still wings, looking down, cackling.

Patrick watched the fins of the sharks with fixed eyes. His lips were drawn back from his clenched teeth. His white eyebrows were raised up on his wrinkled forehead. Suddenly he dropped his oars, took his knife from his pocket and opened it.

Martin's back quivered. He dropped his oars and stood up, uttering a strange, wild shriek. He turned on his brother. Patrick was crouching in the prow, gripping the open knife. They rushed at one another. The boat swung round. The beam, carried on a tall wave, came crashing into it.

The brothers, just as they were about to grapple with one another, saw the beam, with upraised snout, looming over them. They raised their hands and uttered a cry of horror. The knife dropped from Patrick's hands into the sea. They threw their arms around one another in an embrace, as the log fell, smashing them and the boat beneath its weight.

Clasped in one another's arms, they began to sink. The sharks' fins came rushing through the water towards the wreck. Then they dived.

The brothers rose once, still clasping one another in a tight embrace. Then they were tugged sharply downwards and they rose no more.

A mass of weeds gathered around the wrecked boat, with the log, snout upwards, astride it, while seagulls soared all round, screaming.

THE young cow was standing on a hillock within the low stone wall behind which the men were crouching. They peered cautiously at her through the little holes between the loose stones of the wall, watching her rotund sides, her slowly swinging tail, her raised head, her twitching ears that listened nervously.

Slight tremors passed along her sides as something moved within her.

Her red body was brown in the night. The green, deep field was pale under a covering of soft mist. Although the wind was dead calm there was a gentle murmur in the air. The murmur of the sea was distinct from the gentle whisper of the myriad blades of grass that stretched lovingly towards the falling dew.

Far away a curlew called in terror on the slope of the blue hill to the east, startled by the ringing of a horse's steel-shod hoof on a stone.

The bodies of the men were indistinct. Their cold, hard peasant faces had assumed a gentle look. Each soul, watching, hidden by the night from its fellows, shyly felt pity and love, of which it would be ashamed during the coarse human intercourse of the day. A youth's lips were open. Sitting by the wall, he stared sideways into the night, with wondering eyes. The old man with withered hands and glittering eyes who knelt on one knee and gripped a pointed stone was muttering something. The cow was his. A man with a black beard crept, stooping, to the old man and whispered in his ear. All listened.

'It won't be before dawn,' he said.

'Nonsense,' the old man said sharply. 'It will come with the turning of the tide.'

'You know best, Red Michael. But with their first calf they fear the night. It has always been so in my memory.'

'There is truth in that,' whispered a little man in a tam-o'-shanter cap, squatting on his heels. 'With their first calf they fear the night.'

'Silence,' said the old man.

They all listened. The cow had moved. Her muscles, straining beneath her weight, creaked as she moved. They could also hear the swishing of her hoofs, dividing the long pale grass as she dragged them slowly. She arched her tail and bobbing her head up and down, she lashed her open jaws with her yellowish coarse tongue.

'Soon, very soon now,' said the old man. 'She'll lie in the hollow by the cairn of little stones.'

The cow halted, shuddering. A rabbit darted from behind a young thistle, its invisible brown

body betrayed by the vaulting white circle of its
tail. It bounded over a mound and disappeared.
Snorting, the cow smelt the thistle. Then she
shivered along her flanks and moved to the heap of
little stones that were overgrown with sprouting
briars. Those she also smelt. Then she sighed
wearily and turning round three times, she knelt,
arose in terror and then immediately knelt again.
She remained for a few moments, swaying uncertainly on her bent forelegs and then with a loud
groan, she lowered her heavy haunches and lay on
her side.

'Ha,' said the old man, rising hurriedly. 'The
darkness of night cannot go against nature. It's the
moon they feel when the tide's about to turn.'

His muscles also creaked, as he rose, with old age
and rheumatism.

'There is great wisdom truly among the old,' said
the little man in the tam-o'-shanter cap, also rising.

'Be ready with the gad,' said the old man to the
youth.

The youth jumped up and snatched at the little
coil of horse-hair rope that lay beside him.

'We better move up by the fence to the gap,' said
the man with the beard.

'Easy now, easy now,' murmured the old man.
'Move carefully. Hush, what's this?'

They all looked behind them. There was a bare sloping field behind them strewn with white stones. A small flock of sheep were sleeping, lying in a half-circle, with their heads resting on their outstretched thin forelegs, on the brow of the field, where it dipped into a long hollow. Beyond, through the night mist, the dim shapes of the village houses rose against the starlit sky. Down there, there was no murmur and the stars glittered, a myriad of wise heavenly eyes watching the earth.

Over the brow of the field, the figure of a woman approached, a little round head and a slender body widening to the wide circle of her long skirt. She approached stooping, one hand resting on her hip, the other carrying something in a tin can.

'It's herself,' somebody said.

'She should have stayed with her child,' the old man grunted.

'Hey,' he said to her angrily when she approached. 'Who sent you?'

'I came with the meal,' she whispered shyly, glancing timorously at the stooping bodies of the men. 'The old woman sent me. Larry has not come back from fishing.'

'Huh,' said the old man with a show of anger, reaching for the can. 'Let me see. It's a foolish avarice to stay out fishing when his young cow's calving. Still,' his voice softened. . . . 'You are a good woman.'

She was his son's young wife. She handed him the can containing oatmeal and then she took a little bottle from her bosom and handed it to him also.

'She said you might be cold in the night and . . . there's a drop that Pateen, the priest's servant, brought from the town to-day.'

'God bless the givers,' they all said.

The old man took the bottle and pulled the cork. He drank. They all drank, blessing God and the cow that was about to calf. Then the old man said:

'You stay here, Nuala, while we go up to the gap. When we call you, come with the oatmeal.'

She nodded her head. They moved up silently to the gap, a few paces away. She could hear them whispering as they crouched there. She also heard the moaning of the cow, but was afraid to look at her through the holes in the wall. Every little sound startled her and she feared the distance of the clear sky. A sheep rose, cleared her nostrils and began to browse without moving. The queer sound of grass being chopped!

What silence! The daisies had arched their white leaves inwards over their yellow hearts; many leafy ladders, along which the dewdrops slid to the yellow core.

Then she heard the old man, her husband's father, saying in a loud whisper:

'Ha! Listen.'

Turning her head towards them, she listened. She heard nothing but the groaning of the cow and the low chopping of the sheep. All the sheep had now risen and browsed, jerking their heads.

'That's it,' someone said. 'The tide is flowing.'

'It's on the black reef that sound is made,' said the timid voice of the youth. 'Is it, Big Stephen? Tell me. Is it?'

'Silence, boy,' they all said.

Then she heard long waves rolling slowly with a slightly angry noise.

For a long time they waited again in silence. Then suddenly there was a loud murmur among the men. She looked and saw them mounting the gap. A stone fell from one man's grip and pattered downwards to the earth. They all clambered over, dropping with dull sounds into the field and then their feet swished through the grass. 'God be with you, my little hag,' somebody called in a gentle anxious voice to the cow. 'The rope, the rope,' said another. 'Hand it to me. You clumsy fool, undo the knot.' There was an angry oath. She crossed herself.

There was a great babel of voices and stamping of feet. 'Heurta, heurta, my pretty girl,' they cried.

55

'God have mercy on us,' she said, getting to her feet.

She thought of her little baby and of her husband who was at sea among the long waves that rolled slowly. Then a voice:

'Praised be God.'

'Come, woman. Come quickly. Come quickly. Quickly now. Brown girl, brown girl. Steady, my darling.'

She ran, holding her skirt, to the gap and passed the can over the wall to the youth. Then she climbed over. They were around the cow in a circle, looking at something on the grass. The old man was scraping something that floundered, with his long, slowly-moving fingers.

Everybody was talking loudly, joyfully.

'Praised be God,' she said, stooping to look at the beautiful, curly, red body of the floundering calf.

Then they scattered oatmeal on him and turned the dazed cow towards him. They stepped aside. She smelt him and then, ignorant of motherhood, she started in fright, as he lifted his head on his feeble, long neck and then let it drop again. She darted away, snorting, her slack sides heaving wildly.

'Heurta, heurta, my little hag,' murmured the old man, and, with a pretence of stealth, he approached the calf and dragged him away a little, lifting him under the belly.

The calf, wriggling his body, uttered a strange sound, the first sound of life, a weary moan.

Then the cow, uttering a fierce, rapturous, savage cry of love, rushed at the calf. She put her mouth close to his, glaring at him with dazed eyes. Then she shivered. A low moaning sound came from her suddenly, like a cry of great anguish or of great love that cannot satisfy itself. Then mumbling, she put out her coarse tongue and licked his body savagely.

He had a face like an ape. His forehead was wrinkled like that of an ape. His eyes were big and grey, with dead, white rims, utterly without expression. His ears were enormous and outstanding. His nose was short. Its point stuck upwards. His nostrils were like the mouths of little bells. He had flabby lips and a sunken chin. The colour of his cheeks was dark brown, like that of the uprooted earth when it is parched by the sun. His cheeks were dented with innumerable little lines, each line a mark of toil, furrows of pain. His rags were tied about him with cords. His boots were caked with dried earth. On his right shoulder he carried his coat, held limply by a great red hand. His left hand gripped the hanging mane of a horse that trudged beside him. He leaned against the horse's shoulder, his head near the horse's head.

His name was Michael Cassidy. He was thirty years old. He was a farm labourer.

It was after sunset. All day the hot summer sun had scorched the earth. Both horse and man were exhausted with work. From dawn that day they had plodded back and forth through a field, stopping only to eat and drink.

They walked through a narrow lane that led to

their master's farm-house. They made a soft, dull sound as their feet splashed heavily through the dry, loose earth. Sometimes the horse's harness jingled on his shoulder. Sometimes the horse snorted. Sometimes Cassidy cleared his throat and looked about him slowly, with upraised eyebrows and with an expression of pain on his face, disturbed by a wandering, vague thought.

On either side of the lane, tall, flowering hedges hemmed them in. The branches brushed against their bodies and their nostrils were filled with the rich smell of exuberant growth. The brown of the dried, uprooted earth and the dark green of the hedges mingled in a grinning, sinister colour before their half-closed, weary eyes. Birds were singing. Beyond the walls of green hedges there were many other sounds of joy. Carts rumbled. Dogs barked. Cows lowed. People cried out. These sounds, in the calm of evening, heralded the fall of night and they were sweet and soothing and passionate. But they were remote from and alien to these two tired beings, trudging homewards, stupefied with work.

These two could not look above the tops of the hedges at the red blaze in the sky where the sun had set.

They came to a place where another lane cut across the one in which they were walking. There was a woman sitting on the grass, under the hedge, at the corner of the other lane, on the left. Neither Cassidy nor the horse saw her until they were within a few feet of her. Then she spoke.

'Is that you, Mick?' she said.

Cassidy started as violently as if he had been struck. Then he stood still. The horse stumbled against Cassidy, shook his head and then halted, drawing in a deep breath through his nostrils with a hoarse sound. Then both Cassidy and the horse looked at the woman.

She also was very ugly. She had a blotched, heavy, pale face, with a thick nose and big, black, stupid eyes. She wore no hat. Her black hair had been plaited and wound about her poll, but the plait had come loose and it hung across her shoulder, with a hairpin sticking from it. She wore an old grey overcoat that was fastened with safety-pins. There was a little white bundle on the grass beside her. She sat on the grass with her legs folded under her like a Turk. Her hands were crossed limply on her stomach. She looked with a strange, unhealthy fixedness at Cassidy. There was terror in her eyes. Her nostrils twitched. There were deep, vertical lines running from between her eyes to the centre of her forehead.

They stared at one another in silence for nearly a minute. The horse raised his head, stretched out his neck and smelt the woman. Then Cassidy spoke.

'Maggie!' he said in a hoarse whisper. 'Is that you?'

When he spoke, his knees began to tremble. Deep lines came in his forehead. A little light appeared in the iris of each of his eyes. The woman did not reply. She went on staring. Her hands moved on her stomach. The fingers interlaced. Then her hands strained, gripping one another closely.

Then Cassidy frowned. He stiffened himself.

'What the hell are ye doin' here?' he said in a fierce whisper. 'What brought ye? What are ye sittin' there for?'

The woman leaned her head forward, opened her mouth to speak and then remained silent. She shook her head, looked to one side and bit her lip. Then she looked at him. Now there was a terribly malign look in her eyes, a look of morose satisfaction and of hatred. Then she rose slowly to her feet, staggering heavily.

He opened his eyes wide when she reached her full height. His lower lip dropped. She slowly opened her shabby overcoat and exposed a black dress, which was so threadbare that a white garment was visible beneath it. The dress was loose above her stomach. On her stomach it swelled out in a balloonish curve, very taut and unseemly.

61

'Jesus!' he said with great force.

Then he spat, looked about him and wiped his mouth on his sleeve.

She sank to the ground, almost falling. She lay, half on her side with one leg stretched out, staring at him. Her chin was sunk into her fat, loose-skinned neck. Then she groaned and gritted her teeth, struck by a sudden pain. She grasped her swollen breasts and looked about her wildly. Her stomach moved. Something had jumped within it.

He looked away and then raised his face to the sky. His face writhed with pain. He looked even more pitiful than the unseemly woman who lay groaning on the grass. He was so ugly.

The sudden pain left the woman. She turned on him again and said savagely:

'What are ye goin' to do about it?'

He looked at her with equal savagery:

'How do I know?'

'What?' she said. 'What are ye drivin' at?'

'Why do ye come to me? That's what I'm drivin' at. How do you know? There's more men than me in the country.'

She uttered an oath and said:

'Ye know well who did it. What are ye goin' to do about it?'

His eyes fell before her. His thighs went lax. He

62

struck the horse a blow on the chest with his elbow and muttered:

'Lift, damn you.'

The horse moved his left fore-hoof a little farther away. Suddenly the woman began to speak at a great speed.

'You'll have to do something for me,' she said. 'By God! You will. It was your doing, Mick Cassidy, and I swear by the mother of God that no man touched me but you. For the love of God, Mick, have a heart in ye. I dragged myself twenty miles since dawn. Christ! I'm sick. I've been working with this coming on me for the past three weeks. Me time is up now. I daren't go to the doctor or say a word to the missus. She spotted me, I know, for I could see her looking at me. So I told her I was sick and that I had to go home. But where can I go? I can't go home. My brother is married in the house and he gives my mother a dog's life as it is. Only for her old age pension he'd send her to the workhouse. It's the door I'd get from him and his rat of a wife. So I came here to you. God knows I wouldn't if I weren't put to it. Ye told me ye'd stand by me and that I'd come to no harm. Ye'll have to do something for me. What are ye goin' to do about it? Christ! Sure ye wouldn't let a sheep lie in a ditch, sick an' dyin', not to mind a human being. Anyway

. . . By God! I'm desperate, Mick. Ye'll have to do something. There's a law in the land. Ye can't bloody well ruin a girl and then go by, so ye can't. Mother of God! What am I saying? Give us a drink. God! I have an awful pain. Can ye do nothin' for me? For God's sake, Mick, have a heart in ye. Ye won't? Eh? By Christ! I'll swing for ye. I'm desperate.'

She began to rise again, distraught. Then she fell prone, unable to rise. He became terrified.

'Hold on, Maggie,' he said.

He bent down towards her and then stood erect again. He rubbed his hands together slowly. The impulse to murder darkened his face; the brute instinct which urges all animals to slay the useless and sick of their kind. It passed rapidly, in a moment. It was followed by another impulse. He thought of the law and he grew afraid. With his lip quivering, he said to her:

'I can't take ye to the loft. They'd see ye comin' in and anyway . . . Can't ye go into the workhouse?'

She sat up and said wildly:

'The workhouse! God! I'd rather drown myself. What would I do with this when I came out? Ye must do something for me, Mick?'

She uttered the last sentence in a peculiar manner

that made him start and look into the distance. He looked back at her suddenly and started again.

'What?' he said. 'What d'ye mean?'

Her eyes were almost closed, but she looked at him cunningly.

'What?' he said again.

She did not reply. She just looked at him cunningly.

'All right,' he said softly. 'The tinkers that were here are gone since yesterday. We'll go up there.'

'Where?'

'The tinkers' ditch.'

'Isn't that dangerous?'

'What for?'

'Wouldn't I be seen there?'

'An' who's to know yer not a tinker? Sure nobody is goin' to prowl into a ditch after a tinker woman.'

'But wouldn't they hear it?'

'What?'

She pointed towards her body.

'What are ye after?' he said fiercely.

'By Christ!' she said in a fury. 'Ye must do something for me, Mick. Else I'll swing for ye.'

'Shut up or I'll choke ye,' he whispered.

She shrank back against the hedge. He turned

away trembling. He leaned his head against the horse's neck and shuddered. Then he sighed.

'Come on,' he said. 'Can ye walk? Ye came this far, so ye can go a little farther, can't ye? We can't stay here. Somebody might come. It's only a couple o' hundred yards.'

She got up and followed him. The horse tried to turn up the lane towards home, but Cassidy lashed the brute and hauled him along to the right.

They went three hundred yards up a steep slope. They reached a copse of fir trees. There was an opening into it from the lane. A moor stretched beyond the copse to the left. Within the opening there was a patch of bare ground, stamped flat. On the close-cropped, stamped, withered grass, there were circular brown and black patches, burnt out; the marks left by fires. On the old patches, young blades of grass were sprouting. Beneath the hedge there was a wide, dry ditch, half full of leaves. Grey sacks, empty tins, rags and pieces of wood, that were once portions of carts and barrels, were strewn about there. In front of the ditch, there was a thick tree stump, with a few of the lower branches, chopped and naked of bark, sticking from it. Names had been carved on the stump. There was a big iron spike stuck in it. The tinkers used it for tethering their animals.

The place was a good shelter. The trees, in leaf, made a thick roof over it. It was dusky there, silent and sinister.

Cassidy pointed to the ditch and said:

'There you are.'

She looked at him and then she looked at the ditch. She went towards the ditch muttering. She kicked at the dead leaves, smelt them and then threw down her bundle. Then she turned to him and said:

'By God! You'll have to stand by me now. You'll have to do something for me. My time is up.'

'Shut yer gob,' he said. 'Don't make a row. Ye don't want to call in the whole village, do ye? Sit down there and be quiet. I'll leave the horse home and come back. I'll bring ye grub.'

She lowered herself heavily to the bed of leaves, sinking into them. She leaned her head against her right hand and closed her eyes.

'Is there anything ye want?' he said.

She opened her eyes, dropped her lower lip and said sombrely:

'I'll want nothing. It's up to you. It's you got me this way. Ye'll have to do something.'

'Well! Amn't I asking ye?' he said. 'Is there anything ye want?'

'Ach!' she said, dropping her head and closing her eyes.

67

'Ha!' he said.

When he was moving away with the horse, she raised her head and said in a startled voice:

'You had better be sure and come back. Else I'll . . .'

He made no reply, but he struck the horse on the side with his fist. She lay down, closed her eyes and began to sob hysterically.

'It's she all right,' he muttered to himself, going away. 'Maggie Conroy. By the Holy, it is.'

He remembered how it had happened towards the end of September of the previous year. He had met her in a field as he was coming home from work. She was sitting under a hedge doing something. He just came towards her, looking at her. Neither of them spoke. He threw her down. She gasped and fainted. He got up afterwards and hurried away terribly frightened. He had looked back and had seen her, turned over on her face, with her hands stretched out. Next day the same thing happened. She went away to a farmer in the middle of October. Now she was here.

He reached the farmhouse, stabled and fed the horse and then went into the farmyard. He talked a while to his master about the day's work, while he washed his hands at the trough in the yard. He received his food from the woman in the kitchen. When he had eaten, he asked for some milk in a can and a piece of bread, saying he was going out that night with a dog. He went over to his loft over the stable and sat on his trestle bed until it was dark . . . trying to think.

After dark he left the loft bringing the food with him. He went by a path across fields to the ditch. He found the woman asleep.

It was now very dark in the ditch. He sat down near her. He could barely see the outline of her body. He heard her snore and the light rustling of the dead leaves as she moved restlessly in her sleep. There were bats roaming through the trees making a buzzing sound. It was very still and hot. Now and again, branches that had become entwined in their growth broke loose, making a queer, snapping sound. Little animals, scurrying through the trees, dislodged dead pieces of stick. All these sounds terrified him. He touched her and then drew away his hand. Then he looked around him, he became still more terrified of the wood. He shook her.

'Are ye hungry, Maggie?'

She awoke with a start and raised her head.

'What?' she said.

Suddenly he felt pity for her. He wanted to caress her and to say kind things to her. But his face

69

remained brutal and he said nothing. Neither did he caress her.

'You're back,' she said. 'God! I'll die. Jesus, Mary and Joseph!'

Another pain struck her. She groaned and clutched her body.

'I brought ye some grub,' he said.

The feeling of tenderness left him when she groaned. He remembered the cause of these groans and that he must do something for her.

She sat up and bent forward and began to utter weird words, the strange mutterings of a woman in travail.

He became terrified again by these words.

'Hadn't ye better eat something?' he whispered.

'Who asked you?' she said fiercely. 'I didn't ask you. You must do something for me though.'

'For God's sake, Maggie,' he said, going on his knees, 'will ye be easy? Ye put the heart crosswise in me. What's the use o' going on like that? Sure ye can't change what's done. Can't ye be quiet now?'

'You must do something for me,' she repeated stupidly.

Then she reached out her hand towards the can.

'Give me that,' she said. 'Give me a drink.'

He handed her the can of milk and the piece of

bread. She became possessed by a panic of hunger when she saw the food. She devoured it all, glaring about her and making queer sounds. She lay back when she had finished. Then she sat up and looked into the distance and said in a petulant tone:

'I'd love a bar of chocolate, so I would.'

She lay back again.

Suddenly it occurred to him that if she died here, he would get into serious trouble.

'Maggie,' he said. 'Will I go for a doctor . . . or a . . . or a priest?'

'Leave me alone,' she muttered. 'I hate the sight of you. Go away.'

'All right,' he said. 'I will.'

'Don't go,' she cried, sitting up. 'Stay here, Mick. Stay with me. Don't leave me. I'm terrified. The pain I have. God! You'll have to do something for me, though. Don't forget that. Otherwise I'll swing for you.'

She became very excited. She clawed the ground with her hands and began to toss about. He began to cry. Again he felt pity for her. He took her in his arms and whispered to her. But she struck her head against his mouth and bit his shoulder.

'Kill me,' she cried. 'Why don't ye put an end to me life? Gimme poison. God! I want to die. Curse the night I was born.'

Hush, hush,' he whispered. 'Don't shout. You'll be heard.'

'I don't care,' she screamed.

Then she blasphemed against the mother of God in a shrill voice.

He crossed himself and begged God's mother to forgive him and her.

Then she grew quiet. It became very silent in the ditch. Nothing moved. The moon appeared above the wood. Its yellow light crept down through the tangled branches. She began to rave in a low voice. She writhed with pain. She laughed. Her laughter terrified him. He gripped her tight within his arms, whispered to her, kissed her clothes and pressed his cheek against her stomach.

'Let me go,' she growled.

Making a great effort, she seized him by the throat and threw him from her with violence. He fell against the side of the ditch, stupefied. He shut his eyes and covered his ears with his hands, to shut out the sound of the cries she was now uttering.

Then, after a while, he became aware that something strange had happened. She was perfectly still. She was breathing heavily. He opened his eyes and looked at her. Now she was visible, in the yellow moonlight. Her face was towards him. It looked yellow, wan, tired, sinister. She did not speak and yet her eyes spoke to him, saying terrible things. Then he heard a cry. He started. Something had moaned beside her in the ditch. He looked at it. Staring at it, he struggled to his feet. She reached out her hand as if to prevent him from rising.

'Eh?' he gasped.

'Where are ye going?' she gasped. 'What did I tell ye?'

'Eh?'

'See?'

'What?'

'What are ye going to do?'

'Let me alone, damn ye.'

Her eyes held him. They terrified him. Again he looked at the thing that lay beside her in the ditch. For one moment he was possessed of a wild feeling of tenderness and pity for it; but at the next moment, he mumbled a cry of horror and covered his cheeks with his hands. Then he took away his hands, looked at her and hated the thing beside her. Raising his right hand above his head and swinging it as if to ward off a blow he muttered:

'Yes. I know. Let me alone. God strike me dead. I'll do it.'

His own words terrified him and he remained still. He again became aware of her sinister, mad eyes.

'Leave me alone,' he said angrily, but without any force.

He stooped and wiped his hands among the dead leaves. Then he groped about and found a sack. He stopped again.

'What are you doing?' she whispered in a dry voice.

'Have ye got a piece of string?' he said.

She did not reply. Again he heard a moan. He cursed and stepped across her body. He covered the thing with the sack and clutched the bundle fiercely against his chest. Then he strode away hurriedly through the wood.

She closed her eyes and clutched her throat and gasped as he went away. She listened eagerly to the sound of his departing steps. When the sound of his steps died away, she began to tremble. Then she burst into tears.

'God have mercy on me,' she muttered. 'Holy Mother of God, have mercy on me. Oh! Jesus, save me, save me.'

She heard a low cough. She became still. She listened. He was coming back. She sat up hurriedly and peered towards him through the trees. He came crouching towards her. She said nothing, but stared at him with hatred. Her eyes were fixed. There was a deep vertical line between them, reaching half-way up her forehead. He sat down on the edge of the ditch, with his head hanging.

'Where have you been?' she whispered.

He began to wipe his hands on the side of the ditch and remained silent.

'Where have you been?'

'Eh?' he said hoarsely. 'It's in the sack. I stuck it in under the root of a tree in a pool of water.'

There was silence for nearly a minute. Then she whispered in a dry voice:

'You killed my child. You murdered my child.'

He raised his head and gaped at her in amazement, still rubbing his hands against the side of the ditch. She became hysterical.

'Where's my baby?' she cried. 'What did you do with it?'

'Eh? What the . . . didn't you . . . Eh?'

'Curse you. May God . . . Give it to me. Give it to me. Where is it?'

'What? What are you saying? Didn't you . . .'

She staggered to her feet.

'Maggie, Maggie,' he whispered, clutching at her knees. She uttered a savage cry and struck at him rapidly with her palms. He began to blubber, dropped his hold and fell to the ground.

Screaming, she ran out of the ditch, into the lane. He raised his head, stretching out his hands and trying to utter her name, but his tongue clove to his palate. Trying to get out of the ditch, he stumbled and struck his head against the tree stump. That steadied him. He ran away through the wood towards his master's house, crying at intervals:

'Ha! Ha!'

A little after dawn police came to his loft and brought him to the barracks. Maggie Conroy was there with them.

'That's him,' she said coldly, pointing at him. 'Ask him what he done with it.'

'I put it in a sack,' he said to them, 'under the root of a tree in a pool of water. She told me to do something for her.'

They gave him three years' penal servitude.

THE OAR

Beneath tall cliffs, two anchored curraghs swung, their light prows bobbing on the gentle waves. Their tarred sides shone in the moonlight. In each, three stooping figures sat on narrow seats, their arms resting on the frail sides, their red-backed hands fingering long lines, that swam, white, through the deep, dark water.

There was a heavy silence there. There were strange shadows on the gently rolling bosom of the sea. The shadows came from the cliffs. Beyond, the Black Reef looked like a fallen spear, a clear black line with a pointed head. Above, the Drowned Man's Leap stood; a proud cruel cliff with a jutting beak, from which water dripped down its bulging, mossy belly. And round the frail, swaying boats, other shadows crept up from the deep, shapes of sunken rocks, where fishes roamed in lairs and beds of clustering yellow weeds.

There were no fish. The lines, baited with heated limpets, wandered idly through the languid sea. Strange too, although the moon shone fitfully, she wandered alone through the sky. Not a star was seen. The sky had no colour. There was no end to the languid sea, no horizon to its endless rows of slowly rolling waves.

The men sat on their narrow seats in silence, fingering their lines. A little while ago, just before nightfall, an enormous school of bream had come about the boats. They rose like mackerel, even to the water's edge and nosed the air, opening their gauzy red lips, like cormorants flying high in a breeze. As if terrified, they darted round the floating baits and nibbled at the lines. Each boat caught a couple and then they disappeared again. Dogfish came. The men were busy swiping the heads off the brutes with their knives and then throwing their carcases over into the sea. Then the dogfish went away.

Excited by the enormous school of fish, the men waited now, although they did not get a bite. When the tide was full, they thought, the fish would come again.

Their greed made them pay no heed to the ominous silence and to the starless sky that had no colour. If those fish came again, they would fill their boat with them.

Now the tide was full. It became very hot. A man with a short red beard growing on his neck stood up in the prow of the boat farthest to the east. He tightened his belt round his waist. He coughed and shouted to the other boat:

'Are ye getting any bite, Little Martin?'

A voice coughed and answered:

'I think, Red Bartly . . . heh, I think now, that there is something to come out of that sky that has no colour in it, like a mist on a mountain.'

'Aye,' said Red Bartly. 'Maybe. That black reef over there, look at it. Ye'd think it was a long fishing-rod held out that way. And yet, my soul from the devil, by day, it's as broad as a boat is long.'

'Yes, yes,' the men murmured. 'Maybe we'd better pull up.'

But nobody moved, for their greedy imaginations filled their boats again and again from the enormous school of red-lipped fish that had risen like a miracle about them.

Suddenly it became still more silent. As when lead melts and flows in a silver stream, all smooth, so the wavelets melted into the sea's bosom. Now a motionless black floor supported the motionless coracles. Now there was no moon. Now a black mass filled the sky. From afar a bellowing noise came and then a wave simmered over a smooth rock quite near. 'Tchee . . . ee . . . ee,' it said.

From each boat a wild cry re-echoed through the caverns of the mighty cliffs:

'In the name of God, cut. Cut. Oars out. Cut.'

With teeth bared, Red Bartly bounded into the prow of the curragh. He gripped his open knife,

79

blade downwards. With one fierce stroke he cut
the hairy yellow anchor rope. The fragile coracle
shivered like an eased horse eager for the road. With
a gay twirl of her high prow, she swung about to the
east. Already an oar was out astern.

'Haul in the lines,' Red Bartly said.

'Damn the lines,' the others growled. 'Ha!
What's that? Oh, Christ.'

Lightning flashed across the bellying sky, lighten-
ing the air with crooked knives of flame. Across
its path, wild thunder crashed, reverberating. The
leaden sea convulsed, swayed up the cliffs and
moaned receding.

With loud cries, the two crews hammered their
tholepins with sea-smoothed stones. Then they
rowed, having knived their lines and their anchor
ropes.

The oars cut the still-flat sea with a screeching
sound. Red Bartly's curragh was in front. As they
lay back, each crew hissed in unison. The whole
strength of their wild hearts was in each stroke. And
the light black boats, arching their gay prows,
bounded like leaping salmon over the sea.

They rowed eastwards beneath the towering cliffs.
To east and west, within them, long reefs and bas-
tions of jutting rock stood out, chiselled like house-
walls by the might of ancient storms. Southwards

the ocean stretched; now a sloping mountain that had no summit.

Now the silent lightning flashed regularly and thunder followed its shooting rays. The boats lit up, stood out, white and small and then they passed with a rumbling swishing sound of moving oars again into the pitch-dark night.

When the lightning flashed on them the faces of the rowing men were white. But they no longer feared. They were fighting now and they murmured calmly as they rowed, wondering would they reach the rock-bound shore below their village before the sea rose in its fullness. The two boats rowed in a line, a few fathoms apart. And although it was pitch-dark, with ancient skill, they kept them, as straight as a rock-bird's flight, on the ancient course, along which their countless ancestors had rowed. They did not think. Every muscle of their bodies was taut with fierce courage.

Moving at great speed, the two boats reached the promontory of the fort. They passed it. Now they were coming abreast of the ancient fort of Aengus, perched on the cliff-top. Then the sea began to break. The wind came sweeping from the ocean, driving the sea before it. Then a loud cry came from the men.

'She's after us,' they said.

They crossed themselves hurriedly. Then they became silent. The long rolling waves broke into fragments. They became alive. Froth overspread them. They hissed as they clashed and cast their spume into the air. Some swayed and wallowed, towering high. Others raced along, with curved summits, as if consciously fleeing before the wind.

The boats no longer bounded forward. They rocked now, swinging their sterns across each following wave. Now the men did not pull fiercely but cautiously. They measured out half and quarter strokes, saving their boats from the foam-capped, monstrous waves that jumped at them from out the lightning flashes.

Still they passed on, tumbling black specks, past the Swan's Cliffs until they were abreast of the great reef that runs west of the Serpent's Hole. There were breakers there; for though it was full tide, the power of the sea swept its waters back afar, exposing even the black weeds that grow in deep caverns. And over the low-tide rocks, giant and beautiful waves came rolling under a shower of fluttering foam.

Then indeed the men trembled in their boats. Red Bartly shouted out with all his might:

'Strengthen your right hands and keep your faces to the sea. Lay her out.'

Now there was a sea in which heavy rocks could float.

They had to tack out into the wind. Blood burst from beneath their finger-nails and from their nostrils. The two curraghs, now quite close together, faced the sea with almost perpendicular prows. Their pointed beaks and rounded shoulders made them look like big black fish hauled quickly, resisting, over the surface of resisting water, from a distant high bank.

Then with a loud cry they turned again eastwards. Now the boats raced eastwards before the flying wind. They had gone a hundred fathoms when, lo! a mighty wave arose. Lightning flashed on it and on the boats. It arose close behind Little Martin's. As the lightning flashed Red Bartly and his crew saw it standing like a falling cliff over Little Martin's boat. Then the lightning passed. Red Bartly turned to receive the wave. In a moment it was upon them. Its spume filled their boat to the transom. As it passed and their boat fell away in it's wake, lightning flashed again in three successive flashes.

Then indeed they saw a terrifying thing in the wild, enchanted light that spread red over the black sea.

First they saw an upraised oar, raised straight on

high, its handle grasped by an upraised hand. Beneath it, they saw an upraised face in agony. The face looked up, with staring eyes, as if saluting Heaven with his upraised oar.

Then darkness came.

Again the lightning flashed. Again they saw the oar, now hurled aloft sideways. There was no hand grasping its handle.

Again darkness came.

The third time the lightning flashed, they looked and saw nothing but a wall of sea approaching them.

'Turn and save them,' cried one of Red Bartly's crew.

Red Bartley roared:

'Sense comes before courage. Three widows are enough. Row, you devils. Row.'

They passed the jutting reef. They reached the harbour's mouth. Now they rowed steadily making great way, through the rolling seas. Their eyes, against their cunning, life-loving wills, still pierced the darkness behind them.

They saw it once again, when lightning flashed, following them. The waves were tossing it. It stood like a mast and then fell, turning round and round, into the darkness.

Then they heard shouting on the shore.

Up among the wailing women they were dragged.

THE OAR

Hands were about their necks and prayers of thanks-
giving whispered on their kissed cheeks.

But other voices shrieked in despair.

Red Bartly kept repeating in a crazed voice:

'We saw an oar by the Serpent's Reef. Raised up
to Heaven with a hand grasping it. It followed us
and no hand was grasping it.'

THE BLACKBIRD'S MATE

A BLACKBIRD was singing on a bough one morning early in the Spring. From his black voluptuous throat he sent aloft fair music in adoration of the rising sun.

The shining star was pouring down upon the dewy earth myriads of beams that rippled like the laughter of a happy God. Its rays danced on the glossy bellies of the naked trees. They warmed the wet buds that were already bursting on the topmost branches. From the earth sweet vapours rose, the smells of countless plants and herbs that were breathing their first breaths. And loud like the clamour of wild torrents flowing over polished stones in mountain glens, a great chorus of birds made the very air drunk with joy.

Although the blackbird sang in ecstasy there was a strange pathetic cry in every note. His body, trembling on the bough, was calling for a mate.

And then, like a gift from the sun to which he sang, a hen bird dropped gently near him on the bough. She was less dark than he and her plumage did not shine in the sunlight. Her beak was not golden. But she had a beautiful, slender body. When he saw her, she looked good to him and her comeliness aroused a desire in him to spread his

86

wings over her and caress her with all his force. So
he sang his wildest and sweetest notes to charm her
and make her come nearer.

She stretched out her neck and hopped towards
him a little way. Then she became motionless, with
outstretched neck, blinking her little eyes, as if
dazzled by the beauty of his golden beak, his shining
feathers and his voluptuous throat.

Then an overflowing passion made him hoarse
and he ceased to sing. He too stretched out his neck
and blinked his eyes. He spread out his wings and
ruffled the feathers on his rotund breast. Uttering
passionate cries, he trotted towards her. But instead
of receiving him she fluttered upwards to another
bough and then looked down with her head to one
side, as if indignant.

He looked at her stupidly for a little while. Then
his sudden burst of passion left him. He became
subtle like the hen. He chirped and shook himself.
He hopped away, raised his beak and sang a few
notes very arrogantly, as if sending out an invitation
for another hen.

That fetched her. She in turn grew excited and
approached him once more with outstretched neck.
Now he pretended not to notice her. But when she
came quite near and made a little chirping sound, he
again spread his wings and offered himself. Imme-

diately she flew away from him, downwards, and then turning suddenly, she wound like a swallow through the trees. He became furious. Uttering a wild cry that re-echoed through the wood, he set off in pursuit.

They left the wood and followed the course of a stream that was lined with willow trees, until at last she hid in the bank among the wet roots of an overhanging bush. He found her there. She offered no resistance. Beak to beak, chirping, fluttering their trailing-wings, they united by the silent stream. Then they returned to the wood.

Now she followed him like a captive and when he hopped along the ground searching for food, she waited behind until he offered her a morsel, or shook a wriggling worm proudly before her eyes. Later she stood near him on a bough while he sang for her, and when night came she slept beside him in the ivy that grew around an old oak tree.

For many days they wandered through the wood, enjoying their young love without labour or anxiety. For food was plentiful. The hospitable earth opened her pores and offered to their prodding beaks a choice store of worms and insects and young sprouts. Except when he was feeding, the cock spent all day singing and playing with his mate. At dawn he sang when the sunrays were chasing the silent ghoulish shadows of the night. And again at noon he warbled when the sun was high. But his wildest song came with the fall of night, as if he called the departing sun, in fear that it would never shine again.

Then one day the hen bird began to search with great care among the branches of a hawthorn bush. At first the cock bird did not seem to understand her purpose, for he began to chirp and flutter about her as if in play. But she was very serious and not inclined for frolic, so she pecked at him angrily when he brushed against her. Then he stood on a twig and watched her with interest. At last she sat in a little hollow where three branches grew from a single stem, making a cosy nook. She turned around several times in this nook and pressed against the branches with her breast. Then, having finished her examination, she hopped upwards a little way and looked down, cocking her head from side to side very wisely. Then she flew around the bush and entered it very hurriedly from various angles. Then she went to neighbouring trees and bushes and looked about her, taking note of the surroundings. Finally she flew to the ground and hopped about. The cock followed her, uttering little cries, questioning her. She paid no heed to him. Now it appeared that he was the captive, following submissively in her tracks.

When she picked up in her beak a little cake of

moist earth and grass and flew with it to the hawthorn bush he knew what she was about. He also
made a little ball and followed her with it. They had
begun to build a nest.

The making of the nest took a very long time because the hen bird insisted on doing all the design-
ing. Whenever the cock added a piece of moss or a
little chip of a twig, she caught it up and put it somewhere else. The business was carried on very
secretly and both birds made wide circuits with
material in their beaks in order to avoid being seen.
Sometimes their work was interrupted by the necessity for driving away from their bush other birds.
The smaller birds went quickly, but a pair of
thrushes, that were also seeking a home, gave great
trouble and were routed only by constant nagging
that lasted a whole afternoon. Then at last the
framework of the nest was finished. Then the hen
sat in it and began to line it with feathers, until it
looked very beautiful and it was hard to believe that
it had not always been there, or that it had not grown
like a flower, fashioned by some genius of the invisible world. Indeed, so beautiful was it that it was
almost impossible to believe that two little birds
could have made it with their beaks, using their
breasts to plane it and compass its roundness.

Now the hen was very proud indeed. On a tree,

within sight of the bush, she sat beside the cock, while he sang for an hour or more, rejoicing in the nest they had built.

They finished their work just in time, because next morning the hen laid an egg in the nest. She laid three more eggs and then she sat on the nest in a queer posture, as if she were in a swoon, or stricken with some sickness. The cock became still more tender. He fetched her food and roamed about the bush, protecting it from enemies.

For eight days after the hen began to sit on her eggs the sun continued to shine all day. The wood was merry with brilliant light and with the joyous smells of growth. Then the sun disappeared. The sky grew dark. The wind rose. Black clouds passed over the wood, dropping slow tendrils of grey mist from their sagging bellies. The air grew icy cold. At dawn the gloomy earth was covered with frost that closed its pores and drove the insects and worms deep into the soil. There was no food for the birds. Growth ceased and many buds that had been tempted forth by the sun withered on the branches. The blackbird began to sing less gaily. But the hen bird on the eggs still sat with the same look of drowsy happiness in her half-closed eyes.

It grew still more cold. A terrible silence spread through the wood, until the creaking of a branch or the passage of a thrush's wings became a sound of loud degree. The sky was shut out by a mist that had no colour. Then snow began to fall.

A little before dawn the first flakes began to drop in silence from the sky. But they fell so quickly that when daylight spread the earth was covered with an immaculate white coat. The trees assumed strange shapes. On the branches little mounds of snow gathered and then fell with soft thuds to the ground. Their falling was the only sound, for the birds were silent, shuddering in their hiding-places, terrified by the strange white flakes that floated down from the dark sky.

The blackbird sat in the hawthorn bush above the nest on which his mate was sitting. He was terrified, for there was no more food and the wet snow came thudding through the bush on to his mate's back from the topmost branches. And the cold was intense. When day advanced and the snow still kept falling, he left the bush and flew away from the wood, across the fields, until he came to a house. There were many birds there, looking for food that might be cast out on rubbish heaps. But although he flew about for many hours he found nothing. Instead he was almost captured by a cat that lay in ambush behind the door of a shed. So he flew back to the nest. His mate was still there lying on the eggs. Night came. He stayed with her on the bush. She never moved or looked at him, but seemed to be still in a swoon of love.

Next morning the snow still fell. Again no bird sang. The wood was like a desert, with the great white hulks of the trees standing around like mummied ghosts. The blackbird was seized with panic and he tried to induce his mate to desert the nest and fly away with him to the warmth of some shed in the plain. But she refused to move. The little creature was growing stiff with cold and hunger, but she could not leave the eggs that she felt warm against her breast.

The cock flew away again looking for food. He got nothing. He returned to the bush, cold and feeble with hunger. He perched above the nest, uttered a plaintive cry, closed his eyes and fell into a swoon.

He was awakened by a joyous cry that came from a thrush perched on a tree near by. He opened his eyes. Lo! It was morning and the sun was blazing in the sky. The white earth glittered. The melting snow was falling from the trees. Birds began to sing. He himself opened his beak and warbled. Then he looked at the nest. His mate still sat there motionless. He flew out from the bush, fierce with hunger. He left the wood and wandered down among the willows that lined the stream. There, sticking from

93

the bank of the stream, he saw the head of a great worm. He pounced on it and pulled forth a large piece. He placed it on a stone and chopped it in two with his beak. He swallowed a piece and flew back with the remainder wild with joy.

When he reached the nest, he began to chirp and to bob his head, to draw his mate's attention. She did not move. He came nearer and bending down, he dangled the worm before her beak. She did not move. He dropped the worm by her beak on the edge on the nest. She did not move. He stood erect and uttered a queer cry. He bent over her, paused and pecked at her gently. She did not move. Then he hopped back in terror.

Then he rushed at her furiously and prodded her comb. He clawed at her and pushed against her with his breast, until he forced himself down into the nest and pushed her over the brink.

Her stiff body fell like a stone from twig to twig until it struck the earth.

For a few moments the cock sat still on the eggs. Then he felt them icy cold against his breast.

Uttering a piteous shriek he flew headlong from the wood.

Snow was falling. The bare, flat, fenceless road had long since disappeared. Now the white snow fell continuously on virgin land, all level, all white, all silent, between the surrounding dim peaks of the mountains. Through the falling snow, on every side, squat humps were visible. They were the mountain peaks. And between them, the moorland was as smooth as a ploughed field. And as silent, oh, as silent as an empty church. Here, the very particles of the air entered the lungs seemingly as big as pebbles and with the sweetness of ripe fruit. An outstretched hand could almost feel the air and the silence. There was absolutely nothing, nothing at all, but falling flakes of white snow, undeflected, falling silently on fallen snow.

Up above was the sky and God perhaps, though it was hard to believe it; hard to believe that there was anything in the whole universe but a flat white stretch of virgin land between squat mountain peaks and a ceaseless shower of falling snow-flakes.

There came the smell of human breathing from the east. Then three figures appeared suddenly, dark, although they were covered with snow. They appeared silently, one by one, stooping forward. The leading man carried his overcoat like a shawl about his head, with a rifle, butt upwards, slung on his right shoulder and two cloth ammunition belts slung across his body. He wore black top boots. His grim young eyes gazed wearily into the falling snow and his boots, scarcely lifted, raked the smooth earth, scattering the fallen snow-flakes.

The second man wore a belted leather coat, of which one arm hung loose. With the other hand he gripped his chest and staggered forward, with sagging, doddering head. A pistol, pouched in a loose belt, swung back and forth with his gait. There was blood on his coat, on his hand and congealed on his black leggings, along which the melting snow ran in a muddy stream. There was a forlorn look in his eyes, but his teeth were set. Sometimes he bared them and drew in a deep breath with a hissing sound.

The third man walked erect. He wore no overcoat and his head was bare. His hair curled and among the curls the snow lay in little rows like some statue in winter. He had a proud, fearless face, bronzed, showing no emotion nor weariness. Now and again, he shook his great body and the snow fell with a rustling sound off his clothes and off the heavy pack he carried. He also had two rifles wrapped in a cape under his arm; and in his right hand he carried a small wooden box that hung from a leather strap.

They walked in each other's tracks slowly. Rapidly the falling snow filled up the imprints of their feet. And when they passed there was silence again.

The man in front halted and raised his eyes to look ahead. The second man staggered against him, groaned with pain and gripped the other about the body with his loose hand to steady himself. The third man put the wooden box on the ground and shifted his pack.

'Where are we now?' he said.

His voice rang out, hollow, in the stillness and several puffs of hot air, the words, jerked out, like steam from a starting engine.

'Can't say,' muttered the man in front. 'Steady, Commandant. We can't be far now. We're on the road anyway. It should be there in front. Can't see, though. It's in a hollow. That's why.'

'What's in a hollow, Jack?' muttered the wounded man. 'Let me lie down here. It's bleeding again.'

'Hold on, Commandant,' said the man in front. 'We'll be at the Mountain Tavern in half a minute. Christ!'

'Put him on my back,' said the big man. 'You carry the stuff.'

'Never mind. I'll walk,' said the wounded man. 'I'll get there all right. Any sign of them?'

They peered into the falling snow behind them. There was utter silence. The ghostly white shower made no sound. A falling curtain.

'Lead on then,' said the big man. 'Lean on me, Commandant.'

They moved on. The wounded man was groaning now and his feet began to drag. Shortly he began to rave in a low voice. Then they halted again. Without speaking, the big man hoisted his comrade, crosswise, on his shoulders. The other man carried the kit. They moved on again.

The peak in front became larger. It was no longer a formless mass. Gradually, through the curtain of snow, it seemed to move towards them and upwards. The air became still more thin. As from the summit of a towering cliff, the atmosphere in front became hollow; and soon, through the haze of snow, they caught a glimpse of the distant plains, between two mountain peaks. There below it lay, like the bottom of a sea, in silence. The mountain sides sank down into it, becoming darker; for it did not snow down there. There was something, after all, other than the snow. But the snowless, downland earth looked dour and unapproachable.

'It must be here,' the leading man said again. 'Why can't we see it? It's just under the shelter of that mountain. There is a little clump of pine trees and a barn with a red roof. Sure I often had a drink in it. Where the name of God is it, anyway?'

'Go on. Stop talking,' said the curly-headed man.

'Can't you be easy?' muttered the leading man, moving ahead and peering into the snow that made his eyelids blink and blink. 'Supposing this is the wrong road, after all. They say people go round and round in the snow. Sure ye could see it from the other end, four miles away in clear weather, two storey high and a slate roof with the sun shining on it. It's facing this way too, right on the top of the hill, with a black board, "Licensed to Sell." Man called Galligan owns it. I'd swear by the Cross of Christ we must be up on it.'

'Hurry on,' snapped the curly man. 'There's a gurgle in his throat. Jesus! His blood is going down my neck. Why can't you hurry on, blast it?'

'Hey, what place is that?' cried the leading man, in a frightened voice. 'D'ye see a ruin?'

They halted. A moment ago there had been nothing in front but a curtain of falling snow, beyond which, as in a child's sick dream, the darkening emptiness of the snowless lowland approached, tumbling like a scudding black cloud. Now a crazy blue heap appeared quite close. Suddenly it heaved up out of the snow. It was a ruined house. There was a smell from it too. From its base irregular tufts

99

of smoke curled up spasmodically; dying almost as soon as they appeared and then appearing again.

The two men watched it. There was no emotion in their faces. They just looked, as if without interest. It was too strange. The *Mountain Tavern* was a smoking ruin.

'It's gone west,' murmured the leading man.

'Eh?' shouted the curly man. 'Gone did ye say?'

'Aye. Burned to the ground. See?'

'Well?'

'God knows. We're up the pole.'

Suddenly the curly man uttered a cry of rage and staggered forward under his load. The other man opened his mouth wide, drew in an enormous breath and dropped his head wearily on his chest. Trailing his rifle in the snow behind him, he reeled forward, shaking his head from side to side, with his under lip trembling. Then he began to sing foolishly under his breath. There were people around the ruined house. And as the two men, with their dying comrade, came into view, quite close, these people stopped and gaped at them. There was a woman in front of the house, on the road, sitting on an upturned barrel. She was a thin woman with a long pointed nose and thin black hair that hung in disorder on her thin neck, with hairpins sticking in it. She had a long overcoat buttoned over her dress and a man's overcoat about her shoulders. She held a hat with red feathers on it in her right hand, by the rim. Two children, wrapped in queer clothes, stood beside her, clinging to her, a boy and a girl. They also were thin and they had pointed noses like their mother. One man was pulling something out of a window of the ruined house. Another man, within the window, had his head stuck out. He had been handing out something. Another man was in the act of putting a tin trunk on a cart, to which a horse was harnessed, to the right of the house. All looked, gaping, at the newcomers.

'God save all here,' said the curly man, halting near the woman.

Nobody replied. The other man came up and staggered towards the woman, who was sitting on the upturned barrel. The two children, silent with fear, darted around their mother, away from the man. They clutched at her, muttering something inaudibly.

'Is that you, Mrs. Galligan?'

'It is then,' said the woman in a stupid, cold voice. 'And who might you be?'

'We're Republican soldiers,' said the curly man. 'I have a dying man here.'

He lowered the wounded man gently to the ground. Nobody spoke or moved. The snow fell steadily.

'Mummy, mummy,' cried one of the children, there's blood on him. Oh! mummy.'

The two children began to howl. The dying man began to throw his hands about and mutter something. A great rush of blood flowed from him.

'In the name of the Lord God of Heaven,' yelled the curly man, 'are ye savages not to move a foot? Eh? Can't ye go for a doctor? Is there nothing in the house?'

He stooped over the dying man and clutching him in his arms, he cried hoarsely:

'Easy now, Commandant. I'm beside ye. Give us a hand with him, Jack. We'll fix the bandage.'

The two of them, almost in a state of delirium, began to fumble with the dying man. The children wept. The dying man suddenly cried out:

'Stand fast. Stand fast boys. Stand . . .'

Then he made a violent effort to sit up. He opened his mouth and did not close it again.

The woman looked on dazed, with her forehead wrinkled and her lips set tight. The three men who had been doing something among the ruin began to come up slowly. They also appeared dazed, terrified.

'He's gone,' murmured the curly man, sitting erect on his knees. 'God have mercy on him.'

He laid the corpse flat on the ground. The blood still flowed out. The other soldier took off his hat and then, just as he was going to cross himself, he burst into tears. The three men came close and looked on. Then they sheepishly took off their hats.

'Is he dead?' said one of them.

The curly man sat back on his heels.

'He's dead,' he said. 'The curse o' God on this country.'

'And what did ye say happened?'

'Ambush back there. Our column got wiped out. Haven't ye got anything in the house?'

The woman laughed shrilly. The children stopped crying.

'Is there nothing in the house, ye daylight robber?' she cried. 'Look at it, curse ye. It's a black ruin. Go in. Take what ye can find, ye robber.'

'Robbers!' cried the soldier who had been weeping. 'Come on, Curly. Stand by me. I'm no robber. God! Give me a drink. Something to eat. Christ! I'm dyin'.'

He got to his feet and took a pace forward like a drunken man. The curly-headed soldier caught him.

'Keep yer hair on, Jack,' he said.

'Look at what ye've done,' cried the woman. 'Ye've blown up the house over me head. Ye've left me homeless and penniless with yer war. Oh! God, why don't ye drop down the dome of Heaven on me?'

'Sure we didn't blow up yer house,' cried the curly

103

soldier. 'An' we lookin' for shelter after trampin' the mountains since morning. Woman, ye might respect the dead that died for ye.'

The woman spat and hissed at him.

'Let them die. They didn't die for me,' she said. 'Amn't I ruined and wrecked for three long years with yer fightin', goin' back and forth, lootin' and turnin' the honest traveller from my door? For three long years have I kept open house for all of ye and now yer turnin' on one another like dogs after a bitch.'

'None o' that now,' cried the hysterical soldier, trying to raise his rifle.

'Hold on, man,' cried one of the other men. 'She has cause. She has cause.'

He grew excited and waved his hands and addressed his own comrades instead of addressing the soldiers.

'The Republicans came to the house this morning,' he cried. 'So Mr. Galligan told me an' he goin' down the road for McGilligan's motor. The Republicans came, he said. And then . . . then the Free Staters came on top of them and the firing began. Women and children out, they said, under a white flag. So Galligan told me. "They damn near shot me," says he to me, "harbourin' Irregulars under the new act." Shot at sight, or what's worse, they take ye away on the cars, God knows where. Found in a ditch. None of us, God blast my soul if there is a word of a lie in what I am sayin', none of us here have a hand or part in anything. Three miles I came up in the snow when Mr. Galligan told me. Says he to me, "I'll take herself and the kids to aunt Julia's in McGilligan's motor." '

'Where did they go?' said the curly soldier.

'I was comin' to that,' said the man, spitting in the snow and turning towards the woman. 'It's with a bomb they did it, Galligan said to me. Something must have fallen in the fire. They stuck it out, he said. There were six men inside. Not a man came out without a wound. So he said. There were two dead. On a door they took 'em away. They took 'em all off in the cars. And they were goin' to take Mr. Galligan too. There you are now. May the Blessed Virgin look down on here. An' many's a man 'll go thirsty from this day over the mountain road.'

'Aye,' said the woman. 'For twenty years in that house, since my father moved from the village, after buyin' it from Johnny Reilly.'

'Twenty years,' she said again.

'Can't ye give us something to eat?' cried the hysterical man, trying to break loose from the curly soldier, who still held him.

'There's nothing here,' muttered a man, 'until Mr.

Galligan comes in the motor. He should be well on the way now.'

'They were all taken,' said the curly soldier.

'All taken,' said the three men, all together.

'Sit down, Jack,' said the curly soldier.

He pulled his comrade down with him on to the snow. He dropped his head on his chest. The others looked at the soldiers sitting in the snow. The others had a curious, malign look in their eyes. They looked at the dazed, exhausted soldiers and at the corpse with a curious apathy. They looked with hatred. There was no pity in their eyes. They looked steadily without speech or movement, with the serene cruelty of children watching an insect being tortured. They looked patiently, as if calmly watching a monster in its death agony.

The curly-headed soldier suddenly seemed to realize that they were watching him. For he raised his head and peered at them shrewdly through the falling snow. There was utter silence everywhere, except the munching sound made by the horse's jaws as he chewed hay. The snow fell, fell now, in the fading light, mournfully, blotting out the sins of the world.

The soldier's face, that had until then shown neither fear nor weariness, suddenly filled with despair. His lips bulged out. His eyes almost

106

closed. His forehead gathered together and he opened his nostrils wide.

'I'm done,' he said. 'It's no use. Say, men. Send word that we're here. Let them take us. I'm tired fightin'. It's no use.'

No one spoke or stirred. A sound approached. Strange to say, no one paid attention to the sound. And even when a military motor lorry appeared at the brow of the road, nobody moved or spoke. There were Free State soldiers on the lorry. They had their rifles pointed. They drew near slowly. Then, with a rush, they dismounted and came running up.

The two Republican soldiers put up their hands, but they did not rise to their feet.

'Robbers,' screamed the woman. 'I hate ye all. Robbers.'

Her husband was there with them.

'Mary, we're to go in the lorry,' he said to her. 'They're goin' to look after us they said. Fr. Considine went to the barracks.'

'The bloody robbers,' she muttered, getting off the barrel.

'Who's this?' the officer said, roughly handling the corpse.

He raised the head of the corpse.

'Ha!' he said. 'So we got him at last. Eh? Heave him into the lorry, boys. Hurry up. Chuck 'em all in.'

They took away the corpse and the prisoners. There was a big dark spot where the corpse had lain. Snow began to fall on the dark spot.

They took away everybody, including the horse and cart. Everybody went away, down the steep mountain road, into the dark lowland country, where no snow was falling. All was silent again on the flat top of the mountain.

There was nothing in the whole universe again but the black ruin and the black spot where the corpse had lain. Night fell and snow fell, fell like soft soothing white flower petals on the black ruin and on the black spot where the corpse had lain.

PREY

On a Spring morning an old ass was lying on the roadside near a small cottage. He had a grey hide, from which the hair had fallen in many places, leaving brown patches that were glossy with wear and scarred by blows. On his legs there were deep rings, where tethering ropes had eaten into his flesh during years of servitude. His large ears drooped. Lying on his side with his ears thrust out, his belly heaved violently with each slow, raucous breath. His head was erect, but his nostrils almost touched the road. His hot breath poured out on the road and turned into smoke.

Melted snow lay on the road, and here and there was a little crisp flake of melting ice; and the sun was shining brilliantly, for it was a Spring morning and the sun was melting the snow and ice of winter. The road shone. The earth glistened. Birds sang. The air was sharp and penetrating. But everything rejoiced in the cold splendour of the sun-kissed air, except the old ass, that lay on the road, breathing slowly.

A dog came out of the cottage. He raised his tail, barked and rushed at the ass. He stopped near the ass and barked, scratching the road. The ass made a rumbling sound in his throat, a groan. Lowering his head and shaking his ears, he got to his feet. He moved slowly up the road, upwards towards the mountains. The dog followed him, barking. An old man came out of the cottage. He waved his stick and urged on the dog to pursue the ass. That old ass had come up the road last winter and hung around the cottage, trying to rummage food. Nobody seemed to own that ass. Somebody had driven off the useless old tramp and it was a nuisance having him around there, trying to steal food.

'Hulla! Hulla!' said the old man. 'Sick him, Tiger.'

The dog barked. The ass ambled upwards, knocking his forelegs together. He turned around a bend of the road and paused. The dog followed. When the dog turned the corner he stopped barking and stood still. He lowered his tail and began to smell the air in a curious fashion. When the ass saw him do that he shook his head; a gesture of warning. But he did not attack the dog. He set off again, walking slowly upwards and looking behind him sideways at the dog. The dog now had his tail between his legs. He was yawning and licking his jaws. He kept looking behind him cautiously at the cottage. He also kept looking at the ass, slyly, with his snout thrust out. The ass, more hurriedly, but with great labour, rounded another corner. Then the dog, going even more slowly than the ass, followed, with his snout to the ground. He sniffed the ground and thrust out each foot, slowly and noiselessly. He looked from side to side cautiously and in his eyes there was a wild expression.

Suddenly the old man at the cottage whistled. The dog started and ran back with his tail under his belly. Once he halted and smelt the road upwards, where the ass had gone. Then he crawled up to the old man, wagging his tail and dragging himself along the ground on his belly. The old man beat him and spat.

The ass walked upwards until he came to a place where water gushed from a steep bank on the roadside. He put his snout to the white purling fountain of water. He snorted three times. Then he shook himself and tried to drink. It seemed that the water was not to his taste. He shook himself again, lowered his head and moved upwards. He came to the summit of the hill.

Ahead, the white road ran straight across a level moor. There were no houses there. On either side of the moor, little winding paths ran into the moorland. Sheep grazed on the moorland. There were little hills. There were bushes. On the left, in the distance, there was a copse of trees, on the edge of the moor. There was a fence around the trees. The

ass looked at everything. Then he walked off the
road on to the wet grass. He smelt the grass. Then
he turned around three times, groaned and lay on the
grass. He lay on his side. He stretched out his legs
as before. His snout almost touched the ground and
his hot breath poured forth on the grass and turned
into smoke.

Two crows came flying over him. They saw him
lying still on his side with his legs thrust out. They
cawed and wheeled around above in the sky. They
kept cawing. He heard them and groaned. He got
to his feet slowly and moved on, away from the road,
through the moor. The two crows alighted on a bush
and watched him.

Soon his grey figure, moving slowly among the
grey moorland hillocks, became almost invisible.
He halted in many places and looked about him.
But there were several crows following him at a
distance. They no longer cawed. Only when they
lost sight of him did they caw. And again when they
caught sight of him, they became silent. Dropping
their feet and drooping their wings, they let themselves fall slowly, alighting on some small eminence,
at a distance from him. He kept moving on and they
followed him.

Once he came upon a moorland lake, between low
hills. There was a crane standing there among the

rushes. The crane rose languidly, without crying out and flew slowly towards him. It passed over him, looking down intently. It wheeled at a distance and flew back over him, watching intently. It circled the lake and alighted in the same place among the rushes. It began again to look into the water, paying no heed to the ass. The ass moved away, followed by the crows and by a few other strange birds that soared high up in the sky. Now there was a great flock of crows. Some followed. Others went in front. Others fluttered about on either side. He was surrounded on all sides by these black croaking birds.

No matter how he twisted about among the low hills or sheltered beneath bushes, they found him again. Evening came.

The ass came into a little dell that was densely covered by a growth of bushes, briars and gorse. It was a good place, sheltered, quiet. It was inaccessible. There was silence there. It was quite dark. He pushed his way into the centre of it and stood beneath a bush. It was very quiet there. The pursuing birds cawed loudly, at a distance, overhead, on either side. They flew about wildly, cawing. The ass lay down, with his legs to the bush and his head raised against an anthill. He lay still. Tremors passed along his hide, at first gently, then violently. He began to wheeze. The wheeze became a rattling sound. It was very quiet in the dell, beneath the thick growth. It was very dark too. There was perfect peace there. It was a pleasant place to sleep. His hoofs began to tap against the up-lying roots of the bush.

One large bird swooped low over the dell. Passing slowly over the tops of the bushes, it saw the ass lying there beneath, on his side, with his legs thrust out. The bird arose at once, turned around in its flight and cawed querulously. All the birds became still. They all alighted on the ground, round about. They walked to and fro. They prodded the earth. They whetted their beaks.

The ass groaned aloud, stretched out full length, kicked furiously with his hind legs and raised his head. He shivered from head to foot. His head dropped with a thud. His body became still.

With a rustling sound, a hare darted out from the brambles near the ass and fled away, away to the moor. Several other little animals dashed away from the dell and hid themselves in holes. A tiny bird which had come up with something in its beak alighted on a branch near the ass. It bobbed its head. Another little bird alighted beside it, also carrying something in its beak. They both bobbed their heads. Then they both flew away, away, bobbing up and down.

PREY

A crow sprang into the air and wheeled around the dell many times, coming lower and lower. It alighted on the bush above the ass. It preened its feathers. Then it looked down. Without a sound, it let itself fall on to the ass's back. All the birds arose and wheeled round and round the dell.

Later, dogs came and drove away the birds.

THERE was a dark rim round the white disc of the sun. The sky was white, covered with a pale gauze. The sea was white, reflecting the colour of the sky. It was very hot and perfectly still.

The white water of the bay was spotless, except for a round black dot formed by a row-boat. The round, black row-boat lay still, casting no shadow. Not a bird. Not a ripple broke on the low shores, girdled with yellow sand and with grey-black rocks that looked sallow in all this whiteness. Beyond the shore the torrid earth was still, a silent mass of black earth covered with faded, yellow grass, grey rocks, grey stone fences, gleaming granite boulders strewn sparsely, white in the sun.

The tiny fishing-town of Bailenaleice lay in the angle of the bay, facing the bay with its back to the sun. Its hundred houses were scattered round the little square that ended at the pier. To the left of the pier there were a number of fishing hookers, moored side by side, high and dry, with sea grime on their black dry sides.

Ech! The little town was very idle. There had been no fish for a month. What weather!

It was just on the stroke of noon. A small crowd was loafing round the monument, watching the row-boat in silence. They were all drowsy with the heat and their enforced idleness. Here in the square they were at peace, away from their wives who nagged them for their idleness. At a distance, here and there, drowsy voices could be heard, talking aimlessly. Stray dogs rambled about, gambolling in a subdued manner.

There was absolutely no sign of life in the town. The courthouse, the post office, the police barracks, the tiny railhead where a solitary goods waggon was perched on an eminence like a derelict, the drapery shop, the parochial house, where the priest was sitting in his library with his feet on a table reading G. B. Shaw's plays, were all closed, silent and weatherbeaten. In the square itself, the door of the yellow-painted Grand Hotel was closed, and the proprietress, Mrs. Timoney, was leaning on her bare fat elbows at the window of an upper room. The only open door was that of the public-house and grocery shop owned by Mr. Mullally. In the open doorway, Mr. Mullally was sitting on the stone threshold, with his blue waistcoat open on his rotund stomach, half asleep.

Suddenly an enormous man marched down the town towards the pier, striking the earth fiercely with his heavy boots and swinging his arms in an exaggerated manner. The loafers round the monu-

ment jerked their heads around to look at him. Mr.
Mullally also tried to turn his head, but his neck
was so fat that he could not do so. He grunted and
dropped his chin once more. The enormous man
approached, shouting as he did so.

'Now ye divil ye,' whispered one of the loafers in
a tired voice, 'what ails the fellah?'

The man who approached was Bartly Tight, a
farmer. He was dressed in grey frieze from head to
foot. His limbs were enormous, but in spite of their
size his coat and trousers were too large for him.
His coat hung loose about his body and reached
down his thighs. His trousers were wide and doubled
up two or three times at the bottoms. He wore a
very small grey cap at the top of his skull. His head
was large, square and beautifully shaped. His com-
plexion was tanned dark brown, so that he was
almost the same colour as the grey land about him.
A wonderfully handsome giant; so handsome that
all the women in the little town and in the surrounding districts were madly in love with him.

But Bartly Tight was a fanatic and paid no heed
to women. He was a socialist. He had lately returned to the district from America, after his father's
death. Since then he had been trying to convert the
inhabitants to the socialist religion.

'Hey!' he cried, when he reached the square and

caught sight of the loafers. 'Here's a damn' story for you fellahs. Call yourselves Christians, do ye? Why, I'm the only damn' Christian in this blasted town, and I'm an atheist. Search me, fellahs, there's a lot o' bums in this town. Yeh. Know what I'm goin' to tell ye? Ye go to Mass every Sunday an' then rob one another for the rest o' the week.'

'Tell them the old, old story,' cried a loafer, in a sing-song voice, imitating a street preacher.

The others laughed in low voices. Mullally suddenly woke up and he began to giggle. He was so fat and good-natured that he shook all over when he giggled. His little humorous eyes were almost completely hidden behind the layers of flesh on his cheeks. It was very good to look at him laughing. He made no sound. And his great mass of jet black hair shook when he laughed. Tight saw him laughing. He clenched his fist and menaced Mullally with it.

'Yeh,' he cried. 'You can laugh, Mr. Mullally. But you can't put anything over on me. I got your number.'

'Hey, Bartly,' cried a lean man, with a black wart on his face, 'what did ye swally for breakfast that's gone agin yer breath?'

There was another laugh. Bartly looked at the lean man angrily.

The lean man stared very solemnly at Bartly. The tail of his ragged black coat was immersed in the water of the horse trough, on the edge of which he was sitting. Somebody had told him about it an hour before, but he was too lazy to remove it.

'Yeh!' said Bartly to the lean man. 'You're a helluva wit, aren't ye, Micky Degatty. But yer house needs a roof an' ye haven't done a stroke o' work for a year, an' yer wife is –'

'Aw! What odds Bartly?' yawned Micky Degatty. 'Won't we be all dead some day?'

'You put yer finger on the trigger that time all right,' said a dapper little man with a pointed beard, who was leaning his buttocks on a stick. 'Yes. Heh. There's a long rest in the grave for us so we . . . heh . . . we might as well get used to resting. Eh?'

'That be damned,' said Bartly Tight, stamping on the road. 'It's idleness is . . . but that's another story. What I want to know is this. Who knocked the gap in the wall o' my clover field? There's been two donkeys feedin' there all night. 'Twas done deliberate. Who done it?'

'Ha!' said somebody. 'That was a dirty trick.'

'Aw! Begob! A clover field. Was it the red meadow?'

'Ate to the ground,' bellowed Bartly Tight. 'There's Christians for ye. It's not an accident. It's

an old gag in this town. Takin' their cattle around
in the middle o' the night to feed on their neighbour's
land. What? Christians!'

He spat with great vehemence. Everybody began
to discuss the matter with some heat, deprecating
the conduct of the culprit, or culprits, whoever he
or they were. But they soon tired of their interest.
The day was too hot.

'Well,' said an old man at last. 'It's ate now anyway. What's the use talkin' about it? That won't
make the grass grow again.'

'There ye are again!' cried Tight, waving his arms.
'What's the use? What's the use? That's all ye can
say. Let everything go slide. Idleness, ignorance,
immorality. That's what lets ye be a prey to the
whole gang of idle parasites is drinkin' yer body's
blood. Priests, gombeen men, shopkeepers, police,
lawyers. Yah. Why the hell don't ye wake up and
take some interest in social affairs?'

Nobody answered. A dog yawned. Mr. Mullally, for the first time, uttered an audible sound.
Tight turned towards him. Mullally was laughing
with tears flowing down his fat cheeks. Everybody
began to titter.

'Hah!' yelled Tight. 'There he is. The pug-
nosed badger. It's easy for him to laugh. He came
here a few years ago from God knows where, with

his few pounds o' tay in a bag, leavin' them at
people's door-steps. A tay man. Then he buys a
little house an' sets up a shop. Now he's got ye all
in his debt. He's got money in the bank. He's livin'
on ye. What's he done for the town? Nothing. He
ain't a producer. Laugh away, damn ye. Foo!'

Tight was exhausted and he sat down. Nobody
took any notice of him. Mullally just went on laughing. When Tight came to the town first after his
return, people got vexed when he ranted like this.
But a few daring fellows, who took umbrage at his
words and fought him, got such a drubbing from the
giant that now nobody dared to contradict him or
answer him back. And, anyway, he was a gay,
humorous fellow, industrious, clean-living, and the
best of good companions, except on occasions like
this, when a little indiscretion on the part of a thiev-
ing neighbour 'got his goat.'

He sat down. He took out his pipe. He filled it
with tobacco from his pouch. He noticed the row-
boat, which was now moving hurriedly towards the
pier, after having been motionless for at least four
hours.

'Who's that?' he grumbled, waving his tobacco
pouch towards the boat.

'That's Tameen Maloney,' murmured a listless
voice.

'What's he been doin?' grumbled Tight.

'Fishin',' said another listless voice.

Somebody cleared his throat. The dog yawned again and then snapped at a flea. A man who was sitting with wide open mouth suddenly shut his mouth and sat up. He began to cough violently. A fly had entered his wide open mouth.

'Fishin'!' cried Bartly Tight. 'Ha! What's he fishin' for?'

'Mackerel,' said a fat man in a blue sweater, getting to his feet and stretching his hands above his head. 'Give us a pipe-full, Bartly.'

'Go to hell,' said Tight, putting his tobacco in his pocket. 'Go an' earn it. Yer always cadging something. I don't believe in charity. Tobacco is a luxury. I'll give ye a meal if yer hungry, but tobacco – '

'Aw! For God's sake . . .' grumbled the fat man as he shuffled along towards Mullally's shop. 'Hey! Mr. Mullally,' he cried to the shopkeeper in a sullen voice, 'Give us a chew.'

Bartly looked angrily at Mr. Mullaly. Mr. Mullally glanced at Tight, as he took a knife and a square block of tobacco from his pocket. He cut off a piece of the tobacco and handed it to the fat man.

'There ye are!' cried Tight. 'I suppose ye think now ye're a decent fellah. Eh? But ye know yer robbin' that man of his sense of decency. He's just a hanger-on. Bribery an' corruption. That's how ye get them in yer clutches. Put that down on the slate now, Mr. Mullally.'

Mullally giggled again. Suddenly Bartly Tight struck his thigh a violent blow and began to laugh himself.

'Well! I'll be damned,' he cried. 'We're all fools. Eh? It's a funny world. Search me if it ain't. An' . . . after all . . . what were we put into this world for anyway?'

'To save our immortal souls,' said the dapper little man, who was leaning on the stick.

Tight looked at the man keenly, with a merry twinkle in his eyes. The others laughed, knowing that Tight was a bitter opponent of the Church, and expecting him to say something bitter. But Tight just laughed. The heat was overcoming him and with the heat, the laziness engendered by it and the peace of nature, his sense of humour was becoming acute.

'Well,' said another man, 'they say Julius Cæsar, God rest his soul if he had one, couldn't whistle an' chew meal at the same time. So . . .'

'So what?' said Tight.

'I forgot,' said the man, with a long yawn.

They lapsed into silence again, watching the in-coming boat. After a while Bartly Tight spoke again.

'That fellah Tameen Maloney ud make his fortune in a civilized country. Out all mornin' on a day like this. An' all you bums loafin'. Social energy fellah. Eh? That man is a good citizen. Christ! I hope he catches something. I been eatin' salt hash for a month. Not a bite o' fresh stuff in the town, only rotten mutton. Give my two eyes for a roast mackerel off the tongs.'

'Fool!' said the dapper man, sucking his lips and moving towards the pier. 'I can hear the salt cracklin' off its back. My eyes are waterin' for it already.'

'Lashins o' butter on it,' said another man, getting to his feet, 'an' it's food for a bishop.'

'To hell with the bishops,' said Tight, also getting to his feet. 'They should be fed on bad poison.'

They all laughed. Everybody strolled down to the pier. Even Mullally got to his feet and ambled down to the pier. Now it was obvious that he had once been a policeman, because of the way he walked and his splendid black moustaches, that reached out like long thorns on either side of his mouth.

They hailed the boat while it was still a long way off. The boatman did not reply. They watched his bobbing poll, as it rose and fell with the movements of his measured rowing, flush, trup, r-rip, flush. Then he turned round his head and they saw Tameen Maloney's drunken face, all yellow creases, with smuts of grease on the sallow cheeks and shaving scars on his thin jaws. He grounded his boat on the sand to the left of the pier and they saw fish in the boat.

'Bravo, Tameen!' they cried. 'Ye got them.'

'Yuh,' grunted Tameen, getting to his feet in the boat, 'I-I-uh-go-gogotalittle-a-uh-fe-fe-few.'

It was almost impossible to understand a word he said on account of the stoppage in his speech. He had the fish in a little basket, and without mooring the boat he slung the basket on his shoulder and walked up the sand with it hurriedly, on to the pier. Some small boys hauled up the boat for him.

On the pier he went up to Mr. Mullally with the fish.

'Uh-Uh-a-uh-hunerd,' he mumbled.

'Right,' said Mr. Mullally, curtly, 'come along.'

Mr. Mullally had suddenly become a very energetic man. His face had hardened. He was twirling the tips of his moustaches with his fingers and watching the fish greedily.

' Hold on there now,' said Tight, gripping Maloney by the shoulder. 'Lay down that basket. D'ye want to sell yer fish? Eh? If ye do we'll buy it from ye. We don't want any middleman to conduct a transaction."

'Let him go,' cried Mullally, seizing Maloney by

the other shoulder. 'Who's talking about a trans-action? The fish is sold to me.'

Little Tameen Maloney began to stutter. The poor, dirty, ragged, little fellow, gripped by the two giants, was trembling and looked very pitiful. Tight loosed his hold with an oath. Then a very interesting state of affairs was disclosed to the crowd.

It appeared that Tameen Maloney had recently been receiving an occasional drink on credit from Mullally, on the understanding that whatever fish he caught would be handed over to Mullally and that Mullally was to pay whatever he thought fit. Maloney was a confirmed tippler, and he would sell his soul for money if he could find a buyer for it.

It was a very fraudulent arrangement, because Maloney was absolutely penniless, half-starved, and living in deplorable conditions. But the crowd looked upon it as a very trivial affair. They laughed. Tight was the only one who became enraged.

'Well, what did I say?' he cried. 'Look at this barefaced robbery. Christians! Oh! Lord! Ough!'

He spat and walked away, swinging his arms ferociously. Mr. Mullally walked up to his shop with Tameen Maloney. The crowd dispersed, in order to warn their wives that fresh mackerel were to be on sale at Mullally's. The square became quite still.

Presently Mr. Mullally hung up a notice on a piece of cardboard outside his shop. On it was written in scrawling letters: 'Mackerel for Sale. A Penny each. Fine fresh Mackerel.'

Women came rushing from all sides towards the shop to buy the mackerel. The town came to life in an extraordinary fashion. People were running in all directions. The demand was so great that after ten minutes Mr. Mullally came out and changed 'A Penny' to 'Tuppence.' After twenty minutes, when there were only twenty mackerel left, he came out and changed 'Tuppence' to 'Three Pence.' The townspeople began to grumble, but such was the demand for the fish that they paid threepence each for them.

All this time Bartly Tight roamed about his own yard cursing violently. But at last his desire for fresh mackerel got the better of his principles, and he sent his young son down to the shop to buy six mackerel. The little boy got the last six of the fish.

The whole town was frying mackerel. A delicious odour permeated the silent air. Not a soul moved about. Everything was perfectly still. Mr. Mullally was again sitting in his doorway, cutting cheese sandwiches for himself with a large clasp knife. That was his lunch. He was smiling. He had bought the mackerel for two shillings, and he had sold them for nineteen shillings and three pence.

Half an hour passed. Then a stream of sated men strolled into the square once more, their faces red, their stomachs thrust out. They had dined deliciously. They sank wearily to the base of the monument. The same lean man with a black wart on his face sat on the edge of the horse trough and allowed the tail of his ragged coat to become immersed in the water once more. Even Bartly Tight appeared, tamed somewhat by his healthy meal. He also sat down. Nobody spoke. Some closed their eyes and fell asleep. Not a sound was heard, except an occasional grunt and an occasional snore. Mr. Mullally had finished his cheese sandwiches, and he was wearily reading the piece of newspaper in which he had held them.

Then suddenly an extraordinary noise was heard. It came from within Mr. Mullally's public-house. It was almost an inhuman sound, a loud, piercing yell. Strangely enough the crowd of idlers round the monument took very little interest in it. They just glanced towards the shop and smiled. Mr. Mullally himself struggled to his feet and entered his shop, rather hurriedly but not very hurriedly.

'Now ye divil ye,' said a man who was stretched at the base of the monument, 'ye'll see some fun or I'm a liar.'

'Ah!' growled Bartly Tight, staring into the white,

still sea, savagely, 'is there such a thing as pity or are the cannibals right after all? Eh? Are we all cannibals only we don't . . .'

'Ug-ug-g-g . . . r.r.r.r. . . . ya-ah-ah.'

The piercing yell came again and the body of Tameen Maloney was hurled into the yard of Mr. Mullally's public-house. Tameen fell on the yard and writhed there. Mr. Mullally appeared at his door, rubbing one palm against the other.

'He's got em again, the devil,' laughed a man near the monument.

Bartly Tight shuddered, and got to his feet. He spat.

'Blast it,' he said. 'I can't stick this.'

He strode down towards the shore, savagely swinging his arms. It was very hot and still.

Tameen Maloney suddenly jumped to his feet, and began to dance wildly round in a circle, jabbering inarticulately. He had the delirium tremens. He had swallowed two shillingsworth of illicit whisky in the public-house, and then fallen into a stupor. When he awoke from the stupor he was quite mad, temporarily insane. This was quite a usual thing with him. The people laughed.

'Be off now!' shouted Mr. Mullally.

Tameen suddenly frothed at the mouth and ripped a large stone from the coping of the fence. Mr.

Mullally rushed out. Tameen dropped the stone and rushed away. He dived into a little shed farther down. The people got excited. They had never seen him as bad as this. The tremendous heat of the day had evidently intensified his madness. Mr. Mullally got nervous. He retreated hurriedly to his door, shouting as he did so:

'Go for the Civic Guards, Mary Ellen.'

He entered the house and closed the door. The crowd moved over rapidly in the direction in which Tameen had gone. They heard another yell and Tameen appeared with a boat-hook in his hands. He was frothing at the mouth.

'The . . . the . . . the . . . r-r-robber,' he cried. 'Uh-uh-I'll . . . uh . . .'

He rushed at the door and began to batter at it with the boat-hook. The crowd watched, in silence.

In a few seconds two Civic Guards came rushing down the road. They seized Tameen and dragged him up the road to the police barracks. Then the crowd moved away again towards the monument, talking in low voices. The shop door opened again and Mr. Mullally came out to sit on his threshold. For a while there was loud murmuring in various parts of the town. Then the murmuring died down. It was very still and hot.

Down at the point of the long wall that ran into

the sea on the western side of the bay, Bartly Tight was sitting, with his bare feet immersed in the smoothly-rolling white waves.

The white water of the bay was spotless and perfectly still.

THE FALL OF JOSEPH TIMMINS

IT was Sunday evening. Mr. Joseph Timmins sat by his wife's bedside. His wife, Louisa, who had become a confirmed invalid of late, was lying flat in bed, with her shoulders propped against pillows. She was reading aloud an article from *The Irish Rosary*. The article dealt with the 'Persecution of the Church in Mexico.'

Although it was cold outside it was very stuffy in the room. The window was shut and there was a fire. Mrs. Timmins required a warm room for her ailment. It was the heat that first began to make Mr. Timmins discontented as he sat listening. Then the tiresome crackling of the fire made him feel bored and his winter underclothing, which he had just begun to wear, irritated his flesh. Finally he became aware of his wife's rasping and sanctimonious voice and his heart poured out all its rebellious hatred against her.

He stole a glance at her lean, withered, spectacled face, at her clammy yellow hands, at her sunken undeveloped breasts, shaped like a flat board against the bedclothes and he realized acutely that he was fifty years old, without ever having been loved. So a pained dissatisfied expression came into his nervous face and he began to think of her with hatred. Until

133

then he had listened to her reading without grasping the meaning of the words. Now he heard them acutely and hated them, their meaning and the persecuted Church, which represented his unhappiness. The Church was his wife, with her unsexed body and the spectacles on her nose and her horror of the marriage bed.

The sudden upheaval in his mind was all the more violent because it terrified his conscience and he was too weak either to act upon it or to repress it. Indeed he called weakly upon the Blessed Virgin to save him from this sin, but the devil of unrest and concupiscence held his paltry personality within strong chains, so that he heard his thoughts actually shouting in his mind and he sat listening to them, incapable of resistance.

Indecent memories made him flush, and yet they made him hate her all the more and feel ashamed of his cowardice. He remembered how in the first year of their marriage, she had terrified him by her modesty. Yes, she had lain, twenty-five years ago, in that very same bed, their marriage bed. She had turned all the holy pictures to the walls, sprinkled him with holy water and begun to make an act of contrition when the marriage was about to be consummated. It was like being married to a nun or setting up house in a church.

And all these barren years, without children and even without sin. . . . The devil now suggested to his mind, shouted it out, that even sin, strong lustful sin, would have fertilized the arid desert of his life. It would have freed him from her clammy hands and her undeveloped breasts that were shaped against the bedclothes like a flat board.

And he himself . . . what was he? What did he look like in the mirror, one day after his bath, when he saw himself naked? A puny thin man with a beard streaked with grey, a nervous pale face twitching, eyes that had a monk's womanfear in them and bony thighs like an old man.

Word by word, slowly, she enumerated the tortures they were suffering, the bishops and priests of Mexico and her dry lips seemed to find pleasure in the recital of their suffering, in the laceration of their whipped flesh. For their loins had never known a woman. And he, listening, rejoiced wickedly, for those atheists were crashing through the walls of steel that had bound his cowardice and with imaginary bullets he slew hordes of bishops and dashed their gourds of holy water into cesspools and smashed the holy pictures with hammers and spat upon the tablets of contrition. He heard cries of lust and triumph and he mingled with the conquering atheistic soldiers, gouging the eyes of monks and violating nuns.

It was horrible. His irritated skin grew hot and moist with perspiration. He made a sound with his lips, like a hiss of pain. He clenched his hands together and stretched them downwards stiffly towards his thighs.

Suddenly his wife stopped reading, put the magazine on the bed and looked at him. She looked at him down her nose over her spectacles. Her eyes, shining through the fire-brightened glasses, were cold and cruel like the eyes of a miser. They had in them all the meanness and the cruelty and the aridity of perverted sanctity, the joylessness of the woman who has killed her mother instinct, the hatred of the parasitic soul that withers the sap of nature with its clammy touch.

'Joseph,' she said, in her dry, harsh, old-maid's voice, 'is it too much for you, dear?'

Her voice made him start, but he did not look at her. He merely relaxed his hands and let his body go limp. Her voice silenced the devilish voice of rebellion in his mind. Like an automatic machine his conscience registered a mortal sin, the sin of taking pleasure in obscene thoughts. Her voice made him feel conscious of her power over him and of his own weakness. Just as a schoolboy when he hears the voice of the Dean of Studies, remembers his lessons with fear; so Mr. Timmins remembered his work as a director of an insurance company and also the religious societies to which he belonged, especially the one for saving street women 'from the scarlet sin of their unhappy life' as his wife called it. These labours and duties rose up before his mind, big and perpetually unfinished and it became obvious to him that life should mean nothing to him beyond these labours, for which he would be rewarded in the next world.

'Yes,' he said, in a childish feminine voice, 'it's rather horrible, what people . . . I mean . . . things are turning out rather . . . it's unrest, I suppose and . . . science.'

Then he found courage to look at her, because, with a sudden twist, his mind had become like hers, a mind hostile to rebellion and to the desires of the flesh; only with the difference that his mind was more violent and passionate than hers and it would now like to gouge out the eyes of the atheistic soldiers and burn all Protestants and heretics in a big fire. Whereas her mind, behind the cruel cold eyes, watched suffering and torment without movement and saw that they were good.

Her eyes turned wearily and contemptuously from her husband's nervous twitching face. She sighed and said wearily:

'Science, thy name is sin. No, Joseph, it's not

137

science, but the coming of Antichrist. I can feel it in the growing generation. It's truly horrible, but I can even see signs in your nephew that he is becoming a prey to the immoral teachings of the College of Science. He laughs immoderately and yawns when I talk to him of his religious duties. He makes too free with the servants.'

His eyes wandered from her face as she spoke. They rested on her undeveloped breasts that were like a flat board against the bedclothes. In a flash he smelt the sun-baked plains of Mexico and saw bronzed horsemen galloping with screaming nuns on the pommels of their gaudy saddles. 'The curse of the cinema,' she had said. The hot voluptuous sun and the stretching long-grassed golden plains made his flesh throb where the new underclothing grated against it. He shuddered and said almost angrily:

'I am at the end of my patience. Unless he mends his ways. . . . Well, it's hard . . . my dead brother's son . . . and we . . . God didn't bless us with children, but . . . nothing but ruin can come of the company he keeps . . . his drinking and if what I hear is true . . . women.'

'Women,' said Mrs. Timmins, 'you haven't told me anything about . . .'

'My dear,' said Mr. Timmins, 'I didn't want to

disturb . . . I'm not certain and in your condition . . .'

'Joseph,' said Mrs. Timmins. 'You must put your foot down. At once. It's your weakness that's responsible. He must leave the college at once. Take him into your office.'

Mr. Timmins began to speak, but he became inarticulate and he wrung his hands. His face became crimson. He was trying very hard to feel violent against his nephew, but all the time he felt the impact of hot voluptuous sunrays against his irritated flesh and he had visions of wild lawless men in rolling golden plains, herding women.

There was a knock at the door. Then the parlourmaid entered.

'Dinner is served, sir,' she said. 'Will you have your beef-tea now, ma'am?'

'Yes,' said Mrs. Timmins. 'And I think I'll try a little chicken, Kitty. A little breast.'

'Yes, ma'am. Do you want some more coal on the fire?'

'Do.'

While the maid was at the coal-scuttle, Mr. Timmins got up and kissed his wife reverently on the forehead. Her skin was yellow and clammy. His lips quivered as they touched her skin. She called him back from the door, waited until the parlourmaid had left the room and then said in a very severe tone:

'You must speak to him. Don't let me have to do it.'

Then Mr. Timmins went out hurriedly. He hurried without being aware of it, fondling the tip of his little thin beard and moving his lips. When he turned the corner and came to the stairhead he realized the cause of his hurried movements. The parlourmaid was tripping down in front of him. Immediately he flushed and thought of the golden rolling plains, the swishing of the long grass and the flying hoofs of the sweating horses. Everything hot under the boiling sun. His lips grew dry as he went down the stairs in the wake of the comely silken legs and saw, resisting, conscious-striken, the curve of her body and the undulating glossy hair rising from her soft white neck. And he saw that she was young and soft and round and fresh, like a young flower wet with dew, opening out its honeyed cup to a wandering bee.

The maid went off across the hallway towards the kitchen. It was dim there where she disappeared and her tall straight figure, swaying voluptuously at the hips, became alluring among the shadows. When she disappeared something began to burn in his chest, for a few moments only, a pang of mingled joy and sadness. It was queer, both unpleasant and violently intoxicating.

He passed the dining-room door and went into the drawing-room to look for his nephew. The drawing-room was empty. He went through to the dining-room. His nephew was standing at the side-board and he put down something hurriedly that clinked. Mr. Timmins flared up at once.

'Drinking?' he said, in a low tense voice.

The nephew turned round, calmly sticking a coloured handkerchief into his outside breast pocket. He was a young man of twenty, low-sized and powerfully built. His face had already become slightly coarse. His strong neck, his curly dark hair and the contemptuous expression of his grey eyes made him attractive, in the way that stupid, strong men are attractive.

'Hello, Uncle Joe,' he said carelessly in a deep bass voice. 'What's the matter? Everybody takes a pick-me-up before dinner now. I don't feel up to scratch. That match yesterday was a bit tough.'

'I have a few words to say to you, Reggie,' said Mr. Timmins.

'What about?' said the nephew.

The parlourmaid entered with the soup. They took their seats, facing one another across the table. Mr. Timmins watched his nephew's eyes. The nephew smiled slyly at the parlourmaid and he looked at Mr. Timmins with a vacant stare and fiddled with his napkin. As the parlourmaid leaned over his shoulder with the soup, Mr. Timmins again felt that sensation of something burning in his chest. The maid left the room. Mr. Timmins put down his spoon and began to speak furiously.

'She insists on your leaving the College of Science,' he said, 'and I must own . . . well, I quite agree with her. For your father's sake, Reggie . . . Well, I tried my best to . . . give you your own way and to . . . What return do you make? What's going to become of you, I say? Twice during the past week I have been approached by friends. Yes. Mrs. Turnbull stopped me in the street, waved her umbrella in my face and accused you of dragging her Andrew into the ways of the devil. Do you think I hear nothing? I'm told everything, even about your champagne dinner at Jammet's with a common bookmaker.'

The nephew broke bread and said calmly:

'That was on a bet, uncle. Ye can't expect a man . . .'

'A man,' said Mr. Timmins. 'You call yourself a man. I would forgive you for squandering my money if it was for a good purpose. I'm not mean. Your father left me a sacred trust. Lord have mercy on him, his ways were not mine and he died penniless. But I'm not mean. God didn't bless us with children. What I have is yours. But it's a hopeless and miserable end to a life of labour and . . . and self-denial to think that . . . Eh? What's going to become of you? She says I'm weak and it's time. What can I do? Have you no conscience? Football, drink and bad company are no fitting preparation for the . . . Do you or do you not want to?'

The nephew pushed away his empty plate and put his arms on the table.

'Listen, Uncle Joe,' he said calmly.

'Sit properly in my presence,' said Mr. Timmins angrily.

'Oh, all right,' said the nephew, 'ye might let us have a meal in peace. There's something I wanted to ask you about only I'll wait till afterwards. Ye know it's bad for yer digestion talking during meals. I heard Dr. . . .'

'Silence!' shouted Mr. Timmins.

'Very well, only . . .'

'Silence,' whispered Mr. Timmins, blushing and shaking his fist. He heard the maid's footsteps. Mr. Timmins did not look towards the maid. Neither did he think of her. He answered her severely when she asked him if his untouched soup had not been to his liking. He felt a meaningless anger that he had not experienced for years. Hosts of things contributed to produce this anger, trivial things like his new underwear and his wife's yellow skin, weighty things like the consciousness of his own arid years that had never known the softness and subtle passion of love. And he wanted revenge, violent and immediate, a breaking forth that would shatter everything, even his own life and his hope of Paradise.

His appetite was gone, but he wanted to drink. He wanted to go to the sideboard, put a decanter to his lips and spill it down his throat. But he was afraid of his nephew. The young brute. Just like his dead father, who had got drunk on the night after his young wife's funeral and had to be brought home from an improper house.

'He has something to say to me,' thought Mr. Timmins. 'Very well. Nothing he can say will alter my determination to get even with this young ruffian. He's laughing at me. Upon my soul he is.'

Not a word was spoken for the remainder of the meal. The nephew ate ravenously, utterly indifferent to the twitching, angry countenance of his uncle sitting opposite him. Mr. Timmins made a pretence of eating, but each mouthful stuck in his throat. The sound of the maid's footsteps excited him now, just as the contour of her figure had done in the hallway. And under cover of the new silent anger that had hardened his soul, he conceived an extraordinary and intoxicating desire to . . . Each time she bent over him he thought of it with almost diabolical pleasure. There was a soft sweet scent from her hair and even from her white apron when she bent over him. The starched apron crinkled, pressed out of shape by her bending supple figure. He was acutely conscious of every sound and movement she made and of her shape, even though he didn't look at her. When they were finished their coffee, Mr. Timmins said:

'You may leave the table. I'll hear what you have to say in the drawing-room.'

The nephew grunted and went out. Mr. Timmins looked about him stealthily and fondled the tip of his beard. Then he drank two large glasses of port in rapid succession. His head became giddy for a moment. Then he grew exalted. A melancholy sensation that was very pleasant overcame him. Walking very erect, with his hands clasped beneath his shoulder-blades, he went into the drawing-room. The nephew was standing by the fire, leaning his arm on the mantelpiece, with his head bent. He tapped the fender with his toe.

'Well,' said Mr. Timmins.

The nephew looked up and folded his arms.

'I owe some money,' he said. 'It's got to be paid or I'm ruined.'

'Money,' said Mr. Timmins.

'Yes,' said the nephew in a hoarse voice. 'A Jew. He won't wait. I put him off for two months. It's fifty quid.'

Mr. Timmins walked backwards into a chair and sat down.

'Not a cent,' he said, in a calm voice through his teeth. 'Not one penny of my money are you going to get. Do you hear?'

'Very well,' said the nephew, shrugging his shoulders. 'Only he'll come down on you.'"

'Not a penny,' repeated Mr. Timmins.

Suddenly the nephew thrust his head forward and muttered angrily:

'D'ye think it's any pleasure to me to spend yer rotten money or to live in this deadhouse? Why didn't ye let a fellah have a bit o' fun in the house? Where am I to go except to a pub when I want to talk to the lads? There never was anything here only the lives of the saints and novenas to the Holy Ghost an' castin' my father's name at me. God damn the two of ye. Take it or leave it. I know the dodge. But ye're not gettin' me into yer office. I'd rather go to Liverpool and work as a navvy and fry a steak on a shovel. I've got my strength an' I'm not dependin' on you for my lodging.'

Beating his broad chest with his clenched fists and

muttering something under his breath, he walked heavily out of the room and banged the door after him.

For a long time after he had gone, Mr. Timmins sat with his mouth open, without thought. Still without thinking he went into the dining-room and went to the sideboard. He poured out a measure of brandy and tossed it off. He paused, shivered and filled out another measure rather unsteadily. As he was slowly raising it to his lips the maid entered to clear the table. He started and looked her boldly in the face.

Although she had been in the house for six months, this was the first time that he had looked her in the face. The liquor had lent him new eyes and they saw that her face was willing and as bold as his own turbulent desires. She had a handsome face with a skin the colour of milk. Her eyes were quick and passionate. They did not flinch or get excited under his gaze. They were not innocent. Her lips were avaricious. He could bargain with them. He saw and understood all this, because it seemed that the devil had lent him a new brain with the new eyes. He smiled on her. She answered him with another smile and then she said respectfully, as she put a tray on the table:

'I'm afraid you didn't find the dinner to your liking this evening, sir.'

147

Mr. Timmins fluttered his fingers a trifle drunkenly.

'That doesn't matter a bit. Funny, I don't know your name.'

'Kitty, sir.'

'Kitty. Ahem! Yes. Kitty. Isn't there a song "Oh, Kitty, will you marry me?" I think I heard it somewhere.'

The parlourmaid bent her head, shot a glance at him from under her drooping lashes and laughed slyly. Mr. Timmins flushed and tried to laugh also, but his lips were dry. His head became full of hot vapour and his limbs became loose. Without knowing what he was doing, he went towards her and held out his hand. Without looking, she caught his hand and put it away gently from her waist. He left the dining-room, raising his feet high off the floor. He staggered into the arm-chair by the fire in the drawing-room and stared into the fire, contemplating in ecstasy the fantastic visions that swam into his mind through clouds of vapour.

As if to conceal the lovely, sinful visions from his wife, he suddenly became enraged with God and with his neighbours and with the societies of which he was a member. He showered unuttered blasphemies and curses on them all and sneered contemptuously on all the monkish men and skinny women that lived around him in smug, silent houses. He cursed the folly of his past life, his unspent departed youth and the misery of a Heaven in such company. With glee he shattered with a wish all that he had fought to gain in the hereafter, by penance and the curbing of his nature.

And in this mood he became cunning and laughed slyly to himself, seeing the cunning proflicacy of his nephew, as a cunning predatory bee, stealing the honey that fools had gathered and left untouched. And he decided to do likewise, to be cunning also, without belief, a hypocrite, a profligate.

As he rose unsteadily to his feet, he heard a voice say within him:

'My age does not matter. Nor my bony thighs. I have money, I can buy her. Lots of she things. They gave girls to old Solomon.'

He walked to the door leading into the dining-room on tiptoe and saw her bending over the empty tablecloth with a crumb-brush. He made a sound with his lips. She looked up. He smiled. She glanced towards the door that led into the hallway and then looked coldly into his face. He beckoned to her. She did not move and her face looked indignant, but his new cunning saw something in her eyes and lips that made him hurry forward to her round the table. He put his arm round her motionless body and began to whisper into her ear. She kept saying something to which he did not listen, and then he began to shower kisses on her neck, her forehead and her hair. With his trembling hands he pressed her to him, crushing her against the table. And she murmured, struggling to free herself:

'Not here, sir. We'll be seen.'

The door banged. She gasped and broke loose. Dazed, with his arms stretched out, Mr. Timmins looked up. His nephew was standing at the door. The maid was hurrying out the other door into the hallway. The nephew's eyes followed her. Then they turned to Mr. Timmins. Mr. Timmins saw them change slowly from wonder to mocking glee.

In a flash the vapours vanished from his brain and he felt a lassitude in all his limbs. He felt old and weak and helpless and ugly; withered and poor.

'Excuse me, Uncle Joe,' said the nephew. 'I came in to . . .'

'Yes,' interrupted Mr. Timmins, sinking into a chair. 'You came for that money. How much was it, did you say?'

Aɴ old woman named Mary Wiggins got three
goose-eggs from a neighbour in order to hatch a
clutch of goslings. She put an old clucking hen over
the eggs in a wooden box with a straw bed. The hen
proved to be a bad sitter. She was continually desert-
ing the eggs, possibly because they were too big.
The old woman then kept her shut up in the box.
Either through weariness, want of air or simply
through pure devilment, the hen died on the
eggs, two days before it was time for the shells
to break.

The old woman shed tears of rage, both at the loss
of her hen, of which she was particularly fond, and
through fear of losing her goslings. She put the eggs
near the fire in the kitchen, wrapped up in straw and
old clothes. Two days afterwards, one of the eggs
broke and a tiny gosling put out its beak. The other
two eggs proved not to be fertile. They were thrown
away.

The little gosling was a scraggy thing, so small and
so delicate that the old woman, out of pity for it,
wanted to kill it. But her husband said: 'Kill nothing
that is born in your house, woman alive. It's against
the law of God.'

'It's a true saying, my honest fellow,' said the old

woman. 'What comes into the world is sent by God. Praised be He.'

For a long time it seemed certain that the gosling was on the point of death. It spent all the day on the hearth in the kitchen nestling among the peat ashes, either sleeping or making little tweeky noises. When it was offered food, it stretched out its beak and pecked without rising off its stomach. Gradually, however, it became hardier and went out of doors to sit in the sun, on a flat rock. When it was three months it was still a yellowish colour with soft down, even though other goslings of that age in the village were already going to the pond with the flock and able to flap their wings and join in the cackle at evening time, when the setting sun was being saluted. The little gosling was not aware of the other geese, even though it saw them rise on windy days and fly with a great noise from their houses to the pond. It made no effort to become a goose, and at four months of age it still could not stand on one leg.

The old woman came to believe that it was a fairy. The village women agreed with her after some dispute. It was decided to tie pink and red ribbons around the gosling's neck and to sprinkle holy water on its wing feathers.

That was done and then the gosling became sacred in the village. No boy dare throw a stone at it, or pull a feather from its wing, as they were in the habit of doing with geese, in order to get masts for the pieces of cork they floated in the pond as ships. When it began to move about, every house gave it dainty things. All the human beings in the village paid more respect to it than they did to one another. The little gosling had contracted a great affection for Mary Wiggins and followed her round everywhere, so that Mary Wiggins also came to have the reputation of being a woman of wisdom. Dreams were brought to her for unravelling. She was asked to set the spell of the Big Periwinkle and to tie the Knot of the Snakes on the sides of sick cows. And when children were ill, the gosling was brought secretly at night and led three times around the house on a thin halter of horsehair.

When the gosling was a year old it had not yet become a goose. Its down was still slightly yellowish. It did not cackle, but made curious tweeky noises. Instead of stretching out its neck and hissing at strangers, after the manner of a proper goose, it put its head to one side and made funny noises like a duck. It meditated like a hen, was afraid of water and cleansed itself by rolling on the grass. It fed on bread, fish and potatoes. It drank milk and tea. It amused itself by collecting pieces of cloth, nails, small fish-bones and the limpet-shells that are thrown in a heap beside dung-hills. These pieces of refuse it placed in a pile to the left of Mary Wiggins' door. And when the pile was tall, it made a sort of nest in the middle of it and lay in the nest.

Old Mrs. Wiggins had by now realized that the goose was worth money to her. So she became firmly convinced that the goose was gifted with supernatural powers. She accepted, in return for setting spells, a yard of white frieze cloth for unravelling dreams, a pound of sugar for setting the spell of the Big Peri-winkle and half a donkey's load of potatoes for tying the Knot of the Snakes on a sick cow's side. Hitherto a kindly, humorous woman, she took to wearing her shawl in triangular fashion, with the tip of it reaching to her heels. She talked to herself or to her goose as she went along the road. She took long steps like a goose and rolled her eyes occasionally. When she cast a spell she went into an ecstasy, during which she made inarticulate sounds, like 'boum, roum, toum, kroum.'

Soon it became known all over the countryside that there was a woman of wisdom and a fairy goose in the village, and pilgrims came secretly from afar, at the dead of night, on the first night of the new moon, or when the spring tide had begun to wane.

The men soon began to raise their hats passing old Mary Wiggins' house, for it was understood, owing to the cure of Dara Foddy's cow, that the goose was indeed a good fairy and not a malicious one. Such was the excitement in the village and all over the countryside, that what was kept secret so long at last reached the ears of the parish priest.

The story was brought to him by an old woman from a neighbouring village to that in which the goose lived. Before the arrival of the goose, the other old woman had herself cast spells, not through her own merits but through those of her dead mother, who had a long time ago been the woman of wisdom in the district. The priest mounted his horse as soon as he heard the news and galloped at a break-neck speed towards Mary Wiggins' house, carrying his breviary and his stole. When he arrived in the village, he dismounted at a distance from the house, gave his horse to a boy and put his stole around his neck.

A number of the villagers gathered and some tried to warn Mary Wiggins by whistling at a distance, but conscious that they had all taken part in something forbidden by the sacred laws of orthodox religion they were afraid to run ahead of the priest into the house. Mary Wiggins and her husband were within, making little ropes of brown horsehair which they sold as charms.

Outside the door, perched on her high nest, the

little goose was sitting. There were pink and red ribbons around her neck and around her legs there were bands of black tape. She was quite small, a little more than half the size of a normal, healthy goose. But she had an elegant charm of manner, an air of civilization and a consciousness of great dignity, which had grown out of the love and respect of the villagers.

When she saw the priest approach, she began to cackle gently, making the tweaky noise that was peculiar to her. She descended from her perch and waddled towards him, expecting some dainty gift. But instead of stretching out his hand to offer her something and saying, 'Beadai, beadai, come here,' as was customary, the priest halted and muttered something in a harsh, frightened voice. He became red in the face and he took off his hat.

Then for the first time in her life the little goose became terrified. She opened her beak, spread her wings and lowered her head. She began to hiss violently. Turning around, she waddled back to her nest, flapping her wings and raising a loud cackle, just like a goose, although she had never been heard to cackle loudly like a goose before. Clambering up on her high nest, she lay there, quite flat, trembling violently.

The bird, never having known fear of human

beings, never having been treated with discourtesy, was so violently moved by the extraordinary phenomenon of a man wearing black clothes, scowling at her and muttering, that her animal nature was roused and showed itself with disgusting violence.

The people watching this scene were astounded. Some took off their caps and crossed themselves. For some reason it was made manifest to them that the goose was an evil spirit and not the good fairy which they had supposed her to be. Terrified of the priest's stole and of his breviary and of his scowling countenance, they were only too eager to attribute the goose's strange hissing and her still stranger cackle to supernatural forces of an evil nature. Some present even caught a faint rumble of thunder in the east, and although it was not noticed at the time, an old woman later asserted that she heard a great cackle of geese afar off, raised in answer to the fairy goose's cackle.

'It was,' said the old woman, 'certainly the whole army of devils offering her help to kill the holy priest.'

The priest turned to the people and cried, raising his right hand in a threatening manner:

'I wonder the ground doesn't open up and swallow you all. Idolaters!'

'O father, blessed by the hand of God,' cried an old woman, the one who later asserted she had heard the devilish cackle afar off. She threw herself on her knees in the road, crying: 'Spare us, father.'

Old Mrs. Wiggins, having heard the strange noises, rushed out into the yard with her triangular shawl trailing and her black hair loose. She began to make vague, mystic movements with her hands, as had recently become a habit with her. Lost in some sort of ecstasy, she did not see the priest at first. She began to chant something.

'You hag,' cried the priest, rushing up the yard towards her menacingly.

The old woman caught sight of him and screamed. But she faced him boldly.

'Come no farther,' she cried, still in an ecstasy, either affected, or the result of a firm belief in her own mystic powers.

Indeed, it is difficult to believe that she was not in earnest, for she used to be a kind, gentle woman.

Her husband rushed out, crying aloud. Seeing the priest, he dropped a piece of rope he had in his hand and fled around the corner of the house.

'Leave my way, you hag,' cried the priest, raising his hand to strike her.

'Stand back,' she cried. 'Don't lay a hand on my goose.'

'Leave my way,' yelled the priest, 'or I'll curse you.'

'Curse, then,' cried the unfortunate woman. 'Curse!'

Instead, the priest gave her a blow under the ear, which felled her smartly. Then he strode up to the goose's nest and seized the goose. The goose, paralysed with terror, was just able to open her beak and hiss at him. He stripped the ribbons off her neck and tore the tape off her feet. Then he threw her out of the nest. Seizing a spade that stood by the wall, he began to scatter the refuse of which the nest was composed.

The old woman, lying prostrate in the yard, raised her head and began to chant in the traditional fashion, used by women of wisdom.

'I'll call on the winds of the east and of the west, I'll raise the winds of the sea. The lightning will flash in the sky and there'll be great sounds of giants warring in the heavens. Blight will fall on the earth and calves with fishes' tails will be born of cows . . .'

The little goose, making tweeky noises, waddled over to the old woman and tried to hide herself under the long shawl. The people murmured at this, seeing in it fresh signs of devilry.

Then the priest threw down the spade and hauled the old woman to her feet, kicking aside the goose. The old woman, exhausted by her ecstasy and possibly seeking to gain popular support, either went into

159

a faint or feigned one. Her hands and her feet hung limply. Again the people murmured. The priest, becoming embarrassed, put her sitting against the wall. Then he didn't know what to do, for his anger had exhausted his reason. He either became ashamed of having beaten an old woman, or he felt the situation was altogether ridiculous. So he raised his hand and addressed the people in a sorrowful voice.

'Let this be a warning,' he said sadly. 'This poor woman and . . . all of you, led astray by . . . foolish and . . . Avarice is at the back of this,' he cried suddenly in an angry voice, shaking his fist. 'This woman has been preying on your credulity, in order to extort money from you by her pretended sorcery. That's all it is. Money is at the back of it. But I give you warning. If I hear another word about this, I'll . . .'

He paused uncertainly, wondering what to threaten the poor poor with. Then he added:

'I'll report it to the Archbishop of the diocese.'

The people raised a loud murmur, asking forgiveness.

'Fear God,' he added finally, 'and love your neighbours.'

Then throwing a stone angrily at the goose, he strode out of the yard and left the village.

It was then the people began to curse violently and threaten to burn the old woman's house. The responsible people among them, however, chiefly those who had hitherto paid no respect to the superstition concerning the goose, restrained their violence. Finally the people went home and Mary Wiggins' husband, who had been hiding in a barn, came and brought his wife indoors. The little goose, uttering cries of amazement, began to collect the rubbish once more, piling it in a heap in order to rebuild her nest. That night, just after the moon had risen, a band of young men collected, approached Mary Wiggins' house and enticed the goose from her nest, by calling, 'Beadai, beadai, come here, come here.'

The little goose, delighted that people were again kind and respectful to her, waddled down to the gate, making happy noises.

The youths stoned her to death.

And the little goose never uttered a sound, so terrified and amazed was she at this treatment from people who had formerly loved her and whom she had never injured.

Next morning, when Mary Wiggins discovered the dead carcase of the goose, she went into a fit, during which she cursed the village, the priest, and all mankind.

And indeed it appeared that her blasphemous

prayer took some effect at least. Although giants did not war in the heavens and though cows did not give birth to fishes, it is certain that from that day the natives of that village are quarrelsome drunkards, who fear God but do not love one another. And the old woman is again collecting followers from among the wives of the drunkards. These women maintain that the only time in the history of their generation that there was peace and harmony in the village was during the time when the fairy goose was loved by the people.

THE ALIEN SKULL

W HEN he was within ten yards of the enemy
outpost Private Mulhall lay flat, with his
right ear close to the ground. He listened without drawing breath. He strained his ear to catch
a word, a cough or the grating sound of a boot
touching the frost-bound earth. There was no
sound.

Had they gone?

It was eleven o'clock at night. There was perfect
silence along that section of the battle-front. In the
distance there was the monotonous and melancholy
murmur of heavy guns in action. Here everything
was still, as in a tomb. The moon had not risen. But
the sky was not dark. It was an angry, blue colour.
There were stars. It was possible to see the ground
for a long distance. It was freezing heavily. Bayonets,
lying beside dead men, gleamed. All the huddled
figures scattered about between the two lines of
trenches were dead men. There had been a battle
that day.

They had sent out Mulhall to discover whether
the enemy had retired from his front line. If so, an
advance was to be made at midnight into the trenches
evacuated by him. If possible, Mulhall was to bring
back a live prisoner. A man had been seen a little

earlier peering over the top of the advanced post, before which Mulhall was now lying.

Irritated by the silence, Mulhall began to curse under his breath. He ceased to listen and looked back towards his own line. He had come up a slope. He saw the dim shapes of the newly-made scattered posts, the rambling wire fences and the heaps of rooted earth. He cursed and he felt a savage hatred against his officers. He had now been three years at the front without leave. He was always doing punishment behind the line, for insolence and insubordination. In the line he was chosen for every dangerous duty, because of his ferocious courage. But as soon as he came out, he was up again before the adjutant, taken dirty on parade, absent, drunk, or for striking a corporal.

Lying flat on the ground, Mulhall thought savagely of the injustice done to him. He thought with cunning pleasure of crawling back towards his own line and shooting one of the officers or sergeants against whom he had a grudge. With pleasure, he rehearsed, in his mind, this act, until he saw the stricken victim fall, writhe, and lie still. Then terrible disciplinary cries rose up before his mind, his own name shouted out by the sergeant, and then the giant figure of the sergeant-major, with his pace stick under his arm, heels together, erect, reading out

164

the documentary evidence. A whole lot of shouting and stamping and awe-inspiring words. An enormous, invisible, inhuman machine, made of terrible words, constituted in his mind the terror that gave power to his superiors over him.

Compared to that it was pleasant out here.

He turned his head and looked towards the enemy outpost again. His hatred was now directed against the enemy. Their words were meaningless. Whenever he heard their words, they sounded like the barking of a dog. He was not afraid of them, and his punishment was remitted when he killed one or two of them.

Now he ceased to think and he thrust upwards his lower lip. His body became rigid. He fondled the breach of his rifle. With his rifle folded in his arms, ready for use, he slowly pushed his body forward, moving on his left side. He propelled himself with his left foot. He was listening intently. He moved like a snail, a few inches at a time. He made no sound. Then he stopped suddenly when he had gone half the distance. He had heard a sound. It was the sound of teeth gnawing a crust of hard bread, an army biscuit or a stale piece of bread, hardened by the frost. An enemy! There was an enemy there in front, five yards away.

He turned over gently on his stomach and brought

his rifle to the front. Then he slowly touched various parts of his equipment and of his weapon to see that everything was in order. He settled his steel hat a little farther forward on his head, so that its rim shielded his face. Then he raised his back until he was on his elbows and knees. He then raised his feet and hands. He crawled forward as slowly as before and even more silently, breathing gently through his nose. He reached the post and lay still, behind a little knoll that formed the parapet. The enemy was within a yard of him. The enemy snuffled as he chewed at the crust.

Mulhall slowly raised his right knee. He put his right foot to the ground under him. He balanced his rifle in his right hand. He put his left hand on the ground. Then he jumped. He jumped right on top of the man in the hole beyond. But his foot struck something hard as he fell downwards and he tumbled over the man, losing his rifle. His head struck the side of the hole. He was slightly dazed. Almost immediately, however, he raised himself and held out his hands to grope for the enemy.

The enemy had also been tossed by the impact. Just then he was pulling himself up against the side of the hole, his hands supporting him, his mouth and eyes wide open with fright and wonder. There was a piece of black bread in his right hand. There were crumbs of bread on his lips. His face was within a few inches of Mulhall's face.

Mulhall's hands, which he had thrust forward instinctively to grapple with the enemy, instinctively dropped. With the amazing cunning of stupid men, Mulhall saw at a glance that the enemy was much bigger and stronger than himself and that he was almost standing up. Mulhall, on the other hand, was huddled on the ground. Now the enemy was incapable of movement through the paralysis of sudden fear. But if Mulhall touched him the same terror would make him struggle like a madman. Mulhall knew that and lay still. His face imitated the enemy's face. He opened his mouth and dilated his eyes.

They remained motionless, watching one another, like two strange babies. Their rifles lay side by side at the bottom of the hole. The enemy's rifle had been leaning against the side of the hole, and Mulhall had tripped over it, losing his own rifle. Now they were both unarmed. Their faces were so close together that they could hear one another's breathing.

The enemy was a stripling, but fully grown, and of a great size. His cheeks were red and soft. So were his lips. His whole body was covered with good, soft flesh. Mulhall was a squat fellow, thin and hard. His face was pale, and marked with scars. He had eyes like a ferret. A drooping, fair moustache covered his lip and curled into his mouth. He looked brutal, ugly, war-worn, and humpy compared to the fine young enemy, whose flesh was still soft and fresh on his big limbs.

Although his mouth lay stupidly open, as if with terror, Mulhall's mind remained brutal, calm, and determinedly watching for an opportunity to capture the enemy. If he could only reach his gun or disengage his entrenching tool or release his jack-knife. But he must take the fellow alive and drag him back over the frosty ground by the scruff of the neck, prodding him with his bayonet.

Then the enemy did a curious thing that completely puzzled Mulhall. At first his face broke into a smile. Then he laughed outright, showing his teeth that were sound and white, like the teeth of a negro. He made a low, gurgling sound when he laughed. His eyes remained dilated and full of terror while he laughed. Then, slowly, with a jerky, spasmodic movement, he raised the hand that held the crust until the bread was in front of Mulhall's face. Then his face became serious again and his expression changed.

The look of fear left his eyes. They became soft and friendly. His lips trembled. Then his whole body trembled. Gesticulating with his hands and shoulders, he offered the bread to Mulhall eagerly.

168

He moved his lips and made guttural sounds which Mulhall did not understand. Every other time that Mulhall heard those words he thought they were like the barking of a dog. But now they had a different sound.

Mulhall became confused and ashamed. His forehead wrinkled. At first, he felt angry with the enemy, because he had aroused a long-buried feeling of softness. Then he became suspicious. Was the bread poisoned? No. The enemy had been eating it himself. Then he suddenly wanted to shed tears. He thought, with maudlin self-pity, of the brutal callousness and cruelty of his own comrades and superiors. Everybody despised Mulhall. Nobody would share blankets with him in the hut. He always got the dregs of the tea. They moved away from him in the canteen. When he was tied to the wheel of the cookhouse cart, fellows used to jeer at him and cry out: 'Are they bitin' ye, Mull?' With tears in his eyes, Mulhall wanted to bite the hand that held out the bread. The action brought to a climax the whole ghastly misery of his existence. It robbed him of his his only solace, the power to hate somebody whom he could injure with impunity.

He was on the point of striking away the bread when his instinct of cunning warned him. So he took the bread. He fumbled with it uncertainly. Then he stuffed it into the pocket of his tunic. The enemy became delighted and made fresh gestures, gabbling all the while.

Then the enemy stopped gabbling and both became still, watching one another. Their faces became suspicious again. Their eyes wandered over one another's bodies, each strange to the other. Their features became hostile. Their hands jerked uneasily.

Mulhall, slightly unnerved by the enemy's action, began to feel afraid. He became acutely conscious of the enemy's size. So he also began to make guttural sounds imitating the enemy. He touched the enemy's sleeve and said: 'Huh. Yuh. Uh. Uh.' Then he put his finger in his mouth and sucked it. Then he nodded his head eagerly. The enemy looked on in wonder, with suspicion in his eyes.

Mulhall took off his steel hat. There was a crumpled cigarette in the hat. He took out the cigarette and gave it to the enemy.

The enemy's face relaxed again. He was overcome with emotion. He took the cigarette and then kissed Mulhall's hand.

Then Mulhall surrendered completely to this extraordinary new feeling of human love and kindness. Were it not for his native sense of reserve, he would return the enemy's kiss. Instead of that he smiled like a happy child and his head swam. He took the enemy's hand and pressed it three times, mumbling something inaudible. They sat in silence for a whole minute, looking at one another in a state of ecstasy. They loved one another for that minute, as saints love God or as lovers love, in the first discovery of their exalted passion. They were carried up from the silent and frightful corpse-strewn battlefield into some God-filled place, into that dream state where life almost reaches the secret of eternal beauty.

They were startled from their ecstasy by the booming of a single cannon, quite near, to the rear of the enemy lines. They heard the whizzing of the shell over their heads, flying afar.

The enemy soldier started. His face grew stern. He sat up on his heels and took Mulhall's hand. He began to make guttural sounds as he pressed Mulhall's hand fervently.

Mulhall also awoke, but slowly. His soul had sunk deeply into the tender reverie of human love so alien to him. Like a sick man awaking from a heavy sleep, he scanned the enemy's face, seeking the meaning of the change that had been caused by the boom and the whizzing passage of the shell. Slowly he became aware of the boom. Then his cunning awoke in him. Was it a signal?

Without changing his features he became cruel again.

Still uttering guttural sounds, the enemy crawled out into the bottom of the hole and picked up his rifle. Mulhall struggled between the desire of his cunning to throttle the enemy while his back was turned, and an almost identical desire to throw his arms around the enemy's neck and beg him to remain. The cunning desire lost in the struggle and he felt very lonely and miserable as if he were on the point of losing somebody he had loved all his life. So he remained motionless, watching the enemy with soft eyes. And yet he felt violently angry at not being able to hate the enemy and throttle him.

Having taken up his rifle, the enemy paused and looked at the crumpled cigarette which he still held in his hand. Then he smiled and began to make effusive gestures. He kissed the cigarette. Then he made curious sounds, his face aglow with joy and friendship. Then he put down his rifle, pointed to Mulhall's helmet and then to his own. He laughed. He took off his own helmet, which was shaped differently from Mulhall's helmet.

Immediately, Mulhall started violently. He became rigid. All his savagery and brutality again returned. The enemy's skull was exposed. As soon as he saw it the lust of blood overwhelmed him, as if

172

he were a beast of prey in sight of his quarry. The enemy's bare skull acted on his senses like a maddening drug. Its shape was alien. It was shaped like a bullet. It had whitish hairs on it. It was hostile, foreign, uncouth, the mark of the beast. The sight of it caused his blood to curdle in him. A singing sound started in his head, at the rear of his forehead. His eyes glittered. He wanted to kill. He again felt exalted, gripped by the fury of despair.

The skull disappeared. The enemy put his helmet back on his head and then peered over the top of the hole in both directions. Then he struck his chest a great blow, murmured something, and crawled out back towards his own line.

As quick as a cat Mulhall pounced on his own rifle and arranged the breach. Then he crouched up against the side of the hole, thrust out his rifle and looked. The enemy was already a few yards away, slouching off in a stooping position. Quickly, taking quick aim, Mulhall fired. The enemy grunted, stopped, and expanded his chest. Then he turned his head towards Mulhall as he sank slowly. Baring his teeth, with glittering eye, Mulhall aimed slowly at the wondering, gaping young face of the enemy. He fired. The enemy's face twitched and lowered to the ground. His whole body lowered to the ground, trembled and lay still. The haunches remained high off the ground. The feet were drawn up. One hand was thrown out. The head was twisted around towards Mulhall. The face, now stained with blood, still seemed to look at Mulhall with awe and wonder.

Mulhall suddenly felt an irresible desire to run away.

He dashed out of the hole in the direction of his own line, careless of taking cover. He had not gone three yards when he threw up his hands and dropped his gun. He got it right between the shoulder-blades. Coughing and cursing, he fell backwards on his buttocks. His head was still erect. With maniacal joy he looked up into the cruel blue sky and laughed out fierce blasphemies.

They got him again, three times, around the shoulders and neck. His head fell forward. In that position he lay still, like a grotesque statue, dead.

At dawn, when the sun began to shine, he was still sitting that way, like a Turk at prayer, stiff and covered with frost.

JULIA ROGERS lay in bed waiting for her husband to come home. It was long past midnight. The candle at her bedside had guttered out. In the cup of the candlestick the black wick still floated in the warm melted tallow and from the brim of the cup long congealed strings were hanging like stalactites. Books were strewn on the bed. She had been trying to read novels. Now she was propped against the pillows, nervously toying with the figure of a little dove that was wrought in lace on the bosom of her nightgown.

She had a little round face, quite plump, with a slightly darkened upper lip, which gave the impression of a faint moustache. It was, however, devoid of hair. The lip curved upwards and the nose was rather broad at the tip, thus darkening the intervening space, which was unusually short by reason of the lady's excellent breeding. This short, dark, deep, space between mouth and nose gave a peculiar charm to her face in the eyes of a person of taste. Her black eyes and her closely cropped black hair, which had begun to have a greyish tint above the ears, added to this charm. And had her expression been passionate, aggressive and sensual, her face was one that would excite any man to an excess of emotion. But her expression was that of an exceedingly refined woman, thoughtful, reserved and gentle.

Alone in bed, however, the most refined woman exposes her charms in such a manner that the greatest severity of mind is not proof against a suggestion of amorousness. The plump shoulders covered merely by a slight band, the voluptuous shapes of the white breasts heaving against the laced rim of the nightgown at each soft breath and the plump curves of the body half concealed by the disordered bedclothes gave her a disturbing attractiveness which was increased, not diminished, by the nunnish modesty of her expression.

She was thinking of her husband, with a desire of which she felt ashamed and which alarmed her. She had been married six months to him, but as yet they were almost entirely unkown to one another. She was twenty-eight when she married him, a virgin and entirely ignorant of even the most harmless flirtation. The daughter of an eminent scholar, she had been reared in that curious intellectual environment, which in Dublin, is even more remote from actual life than in other University towns. Brought into contact with minds that treated almost every idea and fact with the most calm intellectual complacency, her body had never felt any inclination towards those pleasures of the senses, which women with puritanical training feel with such force. With an almost unmoral mind she developed the physical instincts of a nun. When her father died and she was free to marry, she deliberately chose this hulking fellow Harry Rogers, known as Buster Rogers among his boon companions. He was a famous footballer, an athlete, and a splendid animal. She chose him for that reason, from among the others who offered themselves for the sake of the fortune which she inherited. This choice was due to the cult now in vogue, presumably as the result of our realist literature; the worship of raw nature.

They had never kissed before they married; except one timorous kiss she gave him on the night he proposed to her. They married and she felt an extraordinary revulsion when confronted with the necessity of abandoning herself to him. He appeared so crude, so like an animal. He was a passionate fellow and the reality of passion appeared brutal to her. He, on the other hand, having married her for her money and the social position of her family, pursued her no further after the failure of his first few clumsy approaches. He returned to his other women and to his boon companions. He did not understand her delicacy and he was not subtle enough to awaken the woman in her. He found her insipid.

Women of her acquaintance, as is customary in

Dublin, began to bring her tales of Buster's immoderate conduct. In order to save herself from the contempt of her friends, she persuaded her husband to leave the flat in town and take a bungalow in the mountains. Here matters were even worse. Buster had some sort of a Government position; one of those sinecures that are found for stupid and famous athletes by their admirers. Every morning he left home in his car and returned very late. On Saturday night there was always a celebration and Buster returned home very drunk, usually in a maudlin state. Being a fervent Catholic, he became morbidly repentant in that state. If he had started some fresh amorous adventure or grown tired of an old one, there was always a terrible reaction on these occasions. He cursed, threw things about, called on God to strike him dead for his sins and ended up, sometimes, by rolling over and over on the sitting-room floor, in a state of violent hysteria.

Julia grew desperately lonely. The local doctor, an educated and refined man, was her only consolation. By means of the doctor she tried to make her husband jealous. It was no use. He remained good humoured and inattentive. Every night he peeped into her room, through the door which she always left slightly ajar, said good night in a laughing voice and then retired to his own room. On Saturday nights he slept on the couch in the sitting-room, snoring loudly and muttering in his sleep.

It was very desolating. And Julia had begun to feel that horrible desire for him. How she hated those women! Even the doctor, with his little moustache and his Russian manner of bowing, was of no avail against the extraordinary sensation of being close to this brute of an athlete; possessing him and yet not knowing him.

All this she thought as she lay in bed. And she thought of something else too; something that terrified her even more than her longing for her husband. She was not *quite* sure, but if anything really *did* happen it would be *too* awful.

God! It was impossible to sleep or to lie still. She tossed nervously on her bed, casting off the clothes.

It was a warm June night. The large window was thrown open, admitting the sensuous fragrance of the night through the slightly swaying net curtains. Of an orange colour, the curtains cast the inflowing moonlight in fairy patterns of many hues on the furniture, on the gaily clothed bed, on Julia's seductively disordered figure. Through the pores of the curtains, the starry blue sky and the mountains seemed to look upon her, longing for her in silence; watching her. The slight breeze was like a whisper beckoning her to some mysterious amorous embrace.

The soft warmth of the night and the voluptuous contours of the moonlit heights suggested to her mind the idea of passionate young fairies being out there, thousands of loving fairy couples, lying close together on a bed of moss or heather, lilting their fairy love songs to the moon.

She became terribly ashamed at this and covered her face with her hands. Her cheeks were burning. Then she became afraid. She looked at her watch. It was one o'clock. She became more and more nervous, listened for every sound and started violently when a dog barked in the distance.

At last she jumped out of bed and rang the bell for her servant, rang it violently, before she realized what she had done. A moment later she would have given a fortune not to have rung it. She returned to her bed and pulled the clothes over her head. She waited, panting, hoping the servant was sound asleep. What seemed a long time passed and then she heard a door open. Somebody came shuffling along. It was the servant. There was a knock at the door.

'Come in, Sally,' she said.

A stout woman of middle age came into the room, wearing a night cap and a voluminous night-dress, which, however, did not altogether conceal her figure. She had a rosy face, heavy jaws and merry blue eyes. Her mouth hung open, after the manner of strong-bodied, strong-willed people; people who feel there is no necessity for them to add to the stern power of their jaws by presenting a tight and often deceptive lip to the world. An enormous woman, in fact.

'Oh! Sally,' said Julia, 'I'm awfully sorry. I had a sort of nightmare. I had rung my bell before I knew what I was doing.'

Sally put her candle on the bedside table slowly.

'A nightmare, is it?' she grumbled, still sour on account of her disturbed sleep. 'I was just droppin' off. A book I was readin'.' She shrugged herself. 'A nightmare, did ye say?'

'Do go back to bed, Sally,' said Julia, tapping the woman on the arm gently. 'Forgive me. There's a dear. It's nothing at all. I'm awfully sorry. Go to bed again.'

'A nightmare, did ye say?' said Sally again, sitting on a chair and folding her arms. 'What was it about?'

Julia flushed. Sally was wide awake now and looking at her mistress in the pecularly bold and cunning manner of an old servant looking at a young mistress of whom she is fond, when there is 'something wrong' in the house.

Julia made no answer. Instead she lost her dignity and pouted:

'I wish you'd go to bed, Sally.'

'Himself not home yet?' said Sally.

'No.'

Sally made a sound as if she were tasting something.

'That's a nice way to be,' she grumbled. 'I was twenty years with yer mother, so I was, Lord have mercy on her. That was a happy home, so it was.'

Julia suddenly burst into tears.

'Yer not feelin' well?' said Sally.

There was no reply.

'Will I send word to Dr. Richards in the morning?'

'No, don't. I don't want a doctor. I just feel lonely.'

'No wonder then. He's no great shakes anyway. I don't like that young man at all. So I don't. They don't forget what they hear and what they don't hear they make up. When my old man was alive, God rest his soul, the divil a one he's let . . .'

'What are you talking about?' said Julia sternly.

'And what would you be losing your temper with me for?' said Sally champing her jaws. 'Prut! Wasn't I twenty years with yer mother? "Look after her, Sally," says she to me on her dying bed.

God rest your father, he was a learned man, but soft, very soft.'

'Oh! Don't talk about these things,' said Julia.

Then she broke down again and said:

'Oh! Sally, I feel so miserable.'

'Ha! Ha!' said Sally, fondling her fat arms. 'It's a long time now since I said to meself, "I must step in here an' say a few words." But they say that a wise daughter gets her teeth slowly and a wise woman takes long thought before she speaks. Not that I didn't notice things as they were. This penny boy of a doctor comin' an' goin', leavin' his umbrella in the hall, with little gadgets on it. More a woman than a man. Then himself playin' the rake. It's clear, says I to meself. But there's no use speakin' before it's time. I had a man meself so I had, Lord have mercy on his immortal soul.'

'But what am I to do?' sobbed Jula. 'I've done my best.'

'Prut!' said Sally. 'Anybody could see through that penny boy. He's not going to get jealous of HIM.'

Julia got very tired. Then a cunning look came into her eyes. The eyes of the two women met. Nothing could be more subtle than that meeting of two pair of feminine eyes. Julia's eyes hated the other eyes. Then the older woman sighed and dropped her eyes. Julia's dark upper lip trembled and she looked exceedingly pretty, just like a cat that is purring, not with pleasure but in order to hide her spleen.

'You must beat him,' whispered Sally. 'That's all there's to it.'

Julia's eyes glistened.

'Yes, beat him,' continued Sally. 'I used to beat my old man, nearly every week. He was a gay one too. But he didn't roll on the floor. The crockery he went after. I beat him regular till he died, Lord have mercy on him. Yes, beat him. He's that kind of a man. They respect ye for it. Catch him on the hop and lay on to him. Give it to him as hard as ye can. Wallop him till he cries. He'll cry like a child. I'll stand by ye. And if that doesn't settle him take him into the courts. Otherwise that penny boy of a doctor 'll be the ruination of ye.'

Julia said nothing. She had a look in her eyes, as a cornered cat, beset by dogs, throws her claws into the air and spits. A gentle, purring, pussy cat.

Sally got excited and described in minute detail the proper method of beating a husband. She made minute plans and silenced every attempt at resistance from Julia by stamping her foot and saying 'Prut!' with her fat lips.

They were still talking when Buster drove up to the door in his car.

'Now for it,' said Sally. 'Put on yer dressing gown and wait here.'

She forced Julia out of bed and into her dressing gown. They listened. They heard Buster put the car into the garage. Then the hall door opened and they heard Buster stagger into the hall.

'Holy Moses,' he kept saying in a hoarse voice, 'where am I?'

He went into the sitting-room and pushed things about for some time. He cracked several matches. Then he kicked something with his foot violently. Then he became very still. Then he began to talk, first in a low voice that gradually became a growl and finally became a series of protracted roars.

'Leave me alone,' he began. 'I'll sink with the ship. I'm a sinner. I'm damned. A damned sinner. It ain't my fault. I push my weight. But . . but . . . They won't let me alone. They won't let me alone. I've done it again. Again and again and again. Away with it, boys. Away, away, away.'

'Now's yer time,' said Sally, pushing Julia out into the hall-way.

Julia allowed herself to be pushed to the hall-stand. She accepted the ashplant that was thrust into her hand.

'It's not strong,' whispered Sally, 'but if ye break it, I'll be behind ye with this brassie. This should finish him if he offers to hit back. But ye must do it yerself. Otherwise . . . Go ahead now. He's in the tantrums all right.'

Sally had picked up a brassie from Julia's golf bag that hung on a peg of the hall mirror, when Buster fell to the floor with a loud thud that slightly shook the wooden bungalow. Then his heels tapped on the carpet like the drumsticks of a drummer boy beating a drum.

'Now's the time,' whispered Sally, pushing Julia in front of her. 'Don't hit him on the head though unless he gets vicious. Don't disfigure him. Aim for his back. They hate it most. Makes 'em feel like children.'

They entered the sitting-room through the open door. There was Buster sprawling on the floor, still kicking, clawing the carpet and roaring something that was entirely unintelligible.

He had failed to light the lamp, but he had taken off the shade and flung it on the floor where it remained, smashed into bits. The room, however, was quite light, as a brilliant moonlight streamed in through the two large windows. Buster was wearing evening dress. The moonlight played on his golden curly hair, making it sparkle. The moonlight also gleamed along his back, turning the black a slightly greenish colour. He was quite long in body, but so well built that he appeared plump and round. He had a splendid figure, very masculine and suggestive of great power, a man like a rock, solid, vigorous, as vital as a young stallion.

When he heard the women enter the room, he let go the head of a tiger he had been gripping with his teeth. He turned his face towards them. It was a stupid face, but exciting physically. It was the kind of face that makes women shiver and say to themselves, 'What a brute!' But when approached by the brute they feel a curious lassitude that causes their faces to become wreathed with smiles and their hearts to beat more rapidly. The languor of their bodies belies the angry denial of their words and they fall, half in ecstasy, half in hatred.

Buster raised his head and looked at his wife stupidly. His mouth was wide open and his eyes were almost closed. He looked very funny. Her appearance merely seemed to increase his extraordinary melancholy, for he cried out in a loud voice, 'Jesus of Nazareth,' and struck the floor violently with his head.

'Now, now' muttered Sally excitedly, pushing Julia.

Julia stiffened. She dropped her little hands to her sides, letting her dressing gown hang loosely about her, exposing her bosom. She walked slowly forward, thrusting out her little white feet in their pink high-heeled slippers through the shuffling folds of her dressing gown. Then she gingerly raised the stick when she was quite close to her husband. She stopped dead.

'Prut!' said Sally, standing near the door.

Julia shuddered and took another little pace forward. Buster groaned and gathered himself together in preparation for another monstrous yell. Julia suddenly stepped forward and tipped him ever so gently on the back with the ashplant. Buster immediately became still.

'Prut!' said Sally.

Julia gripped her bosom with her free hand, gasped and struck her husband a fairly smart blow on the same spot, on the small of the back. Buster slowly raised his head, turned his body slightly and looked at his wife. He looked amazed. He wrinkled his brows, as if he were trying to recognize her. He looked exactly like a loutish rustic, come into a town for the first time, standing outside a theatre and gaping at a half-clothed lady of fashion, who is stepping out of her car.

Julia glanced at him. Her expression rapidly changed, until her eyes gleamed brilliantly, her teeth showed, her cheeks became pale and the veins in her neck stood out. She looked wild, ferocious and as maddeningly alluring as only a woman can be, when she is on fire with passion.

'Julia,' murmured Buster in a soft voice.

It was a caress. He had never spoken like that to her. It was the voice of a man seeing a beautiful woman for the first time and completely carried away by a transport of passion.

As soon as she heard him utter her name, a wild excitement took possession of her. Hissing through her teeth, she rained blows on his back. At first she struck with one hand. Then she seized the stick with both hands and struck with all her power, swaying like a peasant woman beetling clothes at a well.

He began to cry out, calling on her to desist. She beat him still more furiously. He uttered a loud yell and turned over on his back. She continued to beat him on the stomach. Then he rolled over again and she beat him on the back once more. At last he began to howl like a dog, making a ludicrous sound. She paused for breath. He gathered himself together and holding up his hands and feet, he cried out:

'Julia, Julia, don't beat me.'

He burst into tears. Gritting her teeth, she swung the stick around her head and struck at him. The stick met his right boot and broke in two pieces with a loud crack.

Julia dropped the broken stick and rubbed her hands. Buster, still weeping, rolled over and over on the floor, endeavouring to get out of her reach. She took a pace forward in pursuit. Then she stopped and sucked her thumb.

'Here's the brassie,' whispered Sally, coming up behind her.

Julia turned on the servant in a furious rage.

'Clear out,' she cried. 'Get back to bed. What are you doing here?'

She grabbed the brassie and pushed the servant out of the room. Sally remonstrated but in a respectful, apologetic manner. There was no trifling with Julia in her present temper. The devil had taken possession of her. Sally shuffled into Julia's bedroom, took her candle and then shuffled off to her own room, holding up her nightdress and muttering under her breath. Julia entered the bedroom, locked the door and then leaned against it, exhausted. Her head fell forward on her shoulders. Her knees were trembling and her throat was dry. But she felt wildly exhilarated. With great joy she listened to the beating of her heart. What had she done? She didn't care. She felt reckless and abandoned and she kept thinking:

'Never again. Never. I'll never suffer again. I'm free.'

Then tears began to flow down her cheeks. She staggered into bed and almost immediately she became terribly afraid. She put the bedclothes over her head and drew up her knees, lying on her side. At any moment she felt the clothes might be pulled off her and something dreadful would happen. Hardly daring to breathe, she listened.

Now there was perfect silence in the house. Not a sound was heard. Soon this silence irritated her. She uncovered her head and thought:

'He's fallen asleep. How perfectly ridiculous!'

This thought deeply mortified her. Now instead of being afraid that something dreadful would happen as the result of her beating him, she became disgusted.

Just as she was again on the point of bursting into tears she heard a sound. It was Buster walking slowly along the corridor and breathing heavily, groaning. She drew in a deep breath and clenched her hands. It seemed to her that in the next few moments her fate would be decided. Would he pass her door?

He stopped. She heard the door handle turned carefully. She smiled in a curious manner. There was a pause. Then she heard:

'Damn it. It's locked. Hey, Julia.'

She didn't reply.

'Say, Julia. Are you asleep?'

She didn't speak, but she tossed on her bed, making the bed creak, in order to let him know that she was awake.

'Why don't you answer me, Julia?' he muttered in an offended, exhausted tone. 'I know you are not asleep. Open the door, can't you, Julia? I . . . I want to explain everything. I can't talk out here, though. Julia. I'm not a dog. I'm a sinner, but I'm not a dog. Julia, I'll go down on my two knees and confess my sins. Give me ONE chance.'

Julia did not speak. She grew excited. He raised his voice a little higher.

'I . . . I wanted to play the game, but I . . . I thought you were fed up with me . . . sorry you married me. I'll go off now, only let me kneel down and confess my sins. Open the door and let me in. I've got my pride. Open the door, I say. Can't you speak to a fellow?'

He waited and received no answer. Julia was sorely tempted to get up and open the door, but she restrained herself with an effort. Buster began to knock on the door, first with his hands and then with his feet. This exertion, and very possibly the sound that he made, had the effect of dissipating his penitent mood. He shouted.

'You're not going to lock me out. I have my rights. I'll break down the door. Down it comes.'

Stepping back, he put his shoulder to the door with all his force. The lock was burst. The door swung open, torn from the top hinge. It hung sideways and Buster fell in a heap on the bedroom floor. Julia became so terrified that she closed her eyes and clutched the bedclothes on her bosom. Groaning, Buster got to his knees and put his hands on the side of the bed. He looked at her.

'Julia,' he whispered, touching her shoulder.

When he touched her, she opened her eyes and looked at him. Their eyes met. His hand tightened its grip on her shoulder. His mouth approached hers. Suddenly he seized her in his arms and embraced her with great violence. Neither spoke.

Soon he was lying beside her, asleep, with his curly golden head resting on her shoulder. She gazed at the head and fondled the hair gently with her palms. Her eyes glowed with tears. They were tears of joy.

The same thought kept running through her head for hours as she lay awake fondling his hair and touching it with her lips:

'Now he will never know that I too am a sinner. He will never know.'

She shuddered in ecstasy at the realization of ALL the happiness which life is capable of giving a woman.

A COUNTRY gentleman, while on a visit to Dublin, received a present of two pet rabbits. He brought them down to his residence in a basket and handed them over to his housekeeper to do what she could with them. He had no interest in the animals and only accepted them through motives of courtesy. The housekeeper grumbled and suggested that they should either be destroyed or sold, observing that rabbits multiplied very rapidly and became a nuisance; but her master said that on no account were they to be disposed of, since he had been made a present of them. So the housekeeper had to put them in the fuel shed, at the rear of the kitchen garden.

The rabbits were quite young and only half-grown. One was of a pure white colour. The other was as black as soot. When they were let loose in the shed, they scurried into a corner and put their heads under one another's bellies, terrified by their unusual surroundings. The housekeeper ordered a boy to gather some cabbage leaves. The leaves were thrown down near the rabbits and the shed was locked for the night.

On the following morning, when the shed was opened, the white rabbit had disappeared. Finding as lit between the wooden wall and the floor of the shed, he had scraped away a hole with his paws and gained his liberty. There were woods near by and he probably reached them. They made no attempt to capture him and the housekeeper was delighted, since it was now impossible for the remaining rabbit to breed on his own account. She also forbade the hole being closed up, hoping that the black rabbit would follow his white comrade.

But the black rabbit did not go away. He had either lost the instinct for freedom or else he was cunning enough to realize that he was safer in the shed that in the wild woods, where he was sure to become the prey of dogs, weasels and sportsmen. Although the hole remained wide open, he never once put his head to it. On the other hand, he made bold with the kitchen garden. As soon as the shed door was opened, he hopped out into the garden and began to nibble at whatever was growing there. Nobody interfered with him and the housekeeper said that it was the master's own loss if the vermin's teeth left the dining-room table without even a stick of celery.

So that, in a short time, the black rabbit grew to an enormous size. He grew until he was bigger than the largest Manx cat. He had enough glossy, jet-black fur on his back to make a bedroom rug. He had teeth like razor blades and ears as long as a hare. The old gentleman used to bring visitors to the library window that overlooked the kitchen garden and point out the rabbit as an interesting monster that was given him as a present.

The housekeeper grew terrified of the animal and said that he was not proper and that he would bring evil to the house. For he developed an amazing precocity. Rabbits are perhaps the most timid and witless of all animals, but this fellow developed character to a surprising degree. If compared to a dog or kitten there was nothing uncanny about him, but compared to other animals of his own species, he was undoubtedly a sport of nature, a sudden upward curve in the direction of perfection and divine intellect; indeed, he was like the first monkey that became inspired with the vision of humanity. And just as all things that become suddenly different and more beautiful than the common herd inspire hatred and fear in the ignorant, so this beautiful, intelligent black rabbit became the hated enemy of the housekeeper.

It was late in the summer before the rabbit reached his full size and began to play tricks. Until then he had amused himself in the ordinary way, feeding assiduously, dashing in and out among the garden plants, turning somersaults on grassy borders when the sun was hot, sitting on his haunches and boxing the air with his forepaws. He lay perfectly flat on the ground with his ears buried in his back and pretended to be invisible. He fled into his shed at great speed on hearing imaginary sounds and he lay on his side with his legs stretched out, pretending to be dead. Then the butterflies arrived and he began to play at a new game. This game he learned from a little poodle dog, which the housekeeper let loose in the garden for an evil purpose.

The master allowed no pet animals of any sort in his house and his hunting dogs were kept chained in another yard. But the housekeeper invited a friend to come to visit her. The friend had a poodle dog. They put the poodle dog in the garden with the rabbit, hoping that he would attack and kill the rabbit or else chase him out into the woods. But when the poodle saw the big rabbit he grew afraid and began to snort. The rabbit hopped up to him out of curiosity. The poodle began to walk backwards, snorting. Suddenly the rabbit snorted also and dashed at the dog. The dog fled howling.

After that the rabbit knew how to snort and amused himself by chasing butterflies and snorting at them. He would lie in hiding beneath a cabbage leaf until a butterfly came near. Then he would jump up and snort. And the butterfly would fly away.

The rabbit became more daring and complex in his activities.

He next amused himself with an overgrown pullet, which had some disease that made it look like a turkey. It had extremely long legs and a round fat body that had hardly any down on it. Generally it stood with its eyes shut and it only woke up to eat the food that was given to it. It could neither scratch the ground nor forage with its beak like an ordinary hen. The rabbit discovered a means of terrifying this fowl and of making its life miserable. He would creep up noiselessly behind it, until he got just between its legs. Then he would snort and toss himself into the air. The pullet would shriek and dash off around the yard with its wings hanging.

Emboldened by this success, the rabbit began to terrify everything that came in his way. Then, one day, while the housekeeper was picking some flowers for the master's table, he concealed himself beneath her skirts and snorted at her also. She uttered a shriek and jumped. She was on the point of swooning with fright and shame at the indelicacy of the occurrence when she saw the rabbit scampering off towards the shed. Then she swore by the Holy Book, master or no master, present or no present, that she would destroy the vermin.

That part of the country is notorious for its cats.

There are hardly any house cats in the district, and if a house cat is brought there it soon goes wild. For the woods are full of cats that are half wild, and when a fresh one of their species comes, they howl around its house until it joins them. In summer they never visit the houses, as game is plentiful. But in winter they become almost tame and very often, if they are allowed, they live around homesteads, destroying the rats and mice.

The housekeeper made friends with one of these wandering cats and she tried to induce him by offers of food to stay in her kitchen. But as it was still early in the autumn, the cat would only stay for an hour or so each day. He drank the proffered milk, warmed himself at the kitchen fire and flew off again.

One day, however, when the cat was lapping milk on the kitchen floor, the black rabbit came hopping into the kitchen. He saw the cat. The cat raised his head and saw the rabbit. They looked at one another. The cat was of a grey colour with whitish rings round his body. He was very ugly and fierce and there were patches of dried mud sticking to his long bedraggled fur. His eyes were shifty like the eyes of a criminal evading pursuit. He looked absolutely evil.

The rabbit surveyed him casually at first and then finding that the cat was afraid, he decided to play a prank. He began to hop towards the cat very slowly. The cat lowered his body. According as the rabbit came nearer, the cat's body sank lower and lower until he was almost flat. Then he suddenly curled into a ball. His hair stood on end and he opened his red jaws. The rabbit was not at all afraid, but kept on hopping closer until at last he grunted and pounced on the cat. The cat yelled and vaulted into the air. He turned in the air and dived for the door. He disappeared out of the door in a flash. The rabbit grunted again and ran after him playfully.

Nothing more was seen of the cat that day. Night fell. The rabbit went into the shed and the shed was locked for the night. The rabbit curled up on his bed of straw and went to sleep.

Then a great howling of cats was heard in the wood close by. The howling sound went to and fro, rising and falling, like the discordant noises of an orchestra operated by madmen. In the darkness, strange lights went among the trees, flashing like phosphorus on the surface of a sea at night. Gradually the wailing, shrieking sounds came closer together until they became one piercing yell. Then they stopped and there was complete silence.

Out of the wood, there came a row of wandering lights, two by two, of lurid colours. They swayed like lanthorns carried in a procession of fairies.

These lights moved and halted and then moved on again, until they reached the shed where the rabbit was asleep. There they formed in a circle and became motionless. The lights were cat's eyes. An army of cats was halted outside the shed.

They remained there quietly for a time without a sound. Then a cat went up slowly to the hole in the wall. He smelt the hole. He looked around at his comrades. He passed his head through the hole three times. He looked again towards his comrades. There was a slight sound, a low, distant, melancholy growl and all the cats made a rolling, swaying movement with their bodies. Then the leading cat dived through the hole and disappeared into the shed. One by one, as silent as ghosts, the other cats did likewise, until they were all in the shed.

There was dead silence for a time. Then there was a loud squeal, a rabbit's squeal of terror. That was followed by a rustling, brushing sound. There was silence again.

The silence was broken by a melancholy chant that rose into the night, evil and despairing, mingled with the crunching sound of flesh being torn.

In the morning, when the housekeeper opened the door of the shed, she saw them sitting in a circle around the rabbit's empty hide.

Their glassy eyes stared at her fearlessly.

I<small>T</small> was a summer afternoon. The clear blue sky was dotted with fluttering larks. The wind was still, as if it listened to their gentle singing. From the shining earth a faint smoke arose, like incense, shaken from invisible thuribles in a rhapsody of joy by hosts of unseen spirits. Such peace had fallen on the world! It seemed there was nothing but love and beauty everywhere; fragrant summer air and the laughter of happy birds. Everything listened to the singing larks in brooding thoughtlessness. Yea, even the horned snails lay stretched out on grey stones with their houses on their backs.

There was no loud sound. Nothing asserted its size in a brutal tumult of wind and thunder. Nothing swaggered with a raucous noise to disarrange the perfect harmony. Even the tiny insects mounting the blades of grass with slow feet were giants in themselves and things of pride to nature.

The grass blades, brushing with the movements of their growth, made joyous gentle sounds, like the sighs of a maiden in love.

A peasant and his family were working in a little field beneath the singing larks. The father, the mother and four children were there. They were putting fresh earth around sprouting potato stalks.

They were very happy. It was a good thing to work there in the little field beneath the singing larks. Yes. God, maybe, gave music to cheer their simple hearts.

The mother and the second eldest daughter weeded the ridges, passing before the others. The father carefully spread around the stalks the precious clay that the eldest son dug from the rocky bottom of the shallow field. A younger son, of twelve years, brought sea sand in a donkey's creels from a far corner of the field. They mixed the sand with the black clay. The fourth child, still almost an infant, staggered about near his mother, plucking weeds slowly and offering them to his mother as gifts.

They worked in silence; except once when by chance the father's shovel slipped on a stone and dislodged a young stalk from its shallow bed. The father uttered a cry. They all looked.

'Oh! Praised be God on high!' the mother said, crossing herself.

In the father's hands was the potato stalk and from its straggling thin roots there hung a cluster of tiny new potatoes, smaller than small marbles. Already their seeds had born fruit and multiplied. They all stood around and wondered. Then suddenly the eldest son, a stripling, spat on his hands and said wistfully:

'Ah! If Mary were here now wouldn't she be glad to see the new potatoes. I remember, on this very spot, she spread seaweed last winter.'

Silence followed this remark. It was of the eldest daughter he had spoken. She had gone to America in early spring. Since then they had only received one letter from her. A neighbour's daughter had written home recently, though, saying that Mary was without work. She had left her first place that a priest had found for her, as servant in a rich woman's house.

The mother bowed her head and murmured sadly:

'God is good. Maybe to-day we'll get a letter.'

The father stooped again, struck the earth fiercely with his shovel and whispered harshly:

'Get on with the work.'

They moved away. But the eldest son mused for a while looking over the distant hills. Then he said loudly to his mother as if in defiance:

'It's too proud she is to write, mother, until she has money to send. I know Mary. She was always the proud one.'

They all bent over their work and the toddling child began again to bring weeds as gifts to his mother. The mother suddenly caught the child in her arms and kissed him. Then she said:

'Oh! They are like angels singing up there. Angels they are like. Wasn't God good to them to give them voices like that? Maybe if she heard the larks sing she'd write. But sure there are no larks in big cities.'

And nobody replied. But surely the larks no longer sang so happily. Now the sky became immense. The world became immense, an empty dangerous vastness. And the music of the fluttering birds had an eerie lilt to it. So they felt; all except the toddling child, who still came innocently to his mother, bringing little weeds as gifts.

Suddenly the merry cries of children mingled with the triumphant singing of the larks. They all paused and stood erect. Two little girls were running up the lane towards the field. Between the winding fences of the narrow lane they saw the darting white pinafores and the bobbing golden heads of the running girls. Their golden heads flashed in the sunlight. They came running, crying out joyously in trilling girlish voices. They were the two remaining children. They were coming home from school.

'What brought ye to the field?' the mother cried while they were still afar off.

'A letter,' one cried, as she jumped on to the fence of the field.

The father dropped his shovel and coughed. The

205

mother crossed herself. The eldest son struck the ground with his spade and said: 'By the Book!'

'Yes, a letter from Mary,' said the other child, climbing over the fence also and eager to participate equally with her sister in the bringing of the good news. 'The postman gave it to us.'

They brought the letter to their father. All crowded round their father by the fence, where there was a little heap of stones. The father sat down, rubbed his fingers carefully on his thighs and took the letter. They all knelt around his knees. The mother took the infant in her arms. They all became very silent. Their breathing became loud. The father turned the letter round about in his hands many times, examining it.

'It's her handwriting surely,' he said at length.

'Yes, yes,' said the eldest son. 'Open it, father.'

'In the name of God,' said the mother.

'God send us good news,' the father said, slowly tearing the envelope.

Then he paused again, afraid to look into the envelope. Then one of the girls said:

'Look, look. There's a cheque in it. I see it against the sun.'

'Eh?' said the mother.

With a rapid movement the father drew out the contents of the envelope. A cheque was within the folded letter. Not a word was spoken until he held up the cheque and said:

'Great God, it's for twenty pounds.'

'My darling,' the mother said, raising her eyes to the sky. 'My treasure, I bore you in my womb. My own sweet treasure.'

The children began to laugh, hysterical with joy. The father coughed and said in a low voice:

'There's a horse for that money to be had. A horse.'

'Oh! Father,' said the eldest son. 'A two-year-old and we'll break it on the strand. I'll break it, father. Then we'll have a horse like the people of the village. Isn't Mary great? Didn't I say she was waiting until she had money to send? A real horse!'

'And then I can have the ass for myself, daddy,' said the second boy.

And he yelled with joy.

'Be quiet will ye,' said the mother quietly in a sad tone. 'Isn't there a letter from my darling? Won't ye read me the letter?'

'Here,' said the father. 'Take it and read it one of ye. My hand is shaking.'

It was shaking and there were tears in his eyes, so that he could see nothing but a blur.

'I'll read it,' said the second daughter.

She took the letter, glanced over it from side to side and then suddenly burst into tears.

'What is it?' said the eldest son angrily. 'Give it to me.'

He took the letter, glanced over it and then his face became stern. All their faces became stern.

'Read it, son,' the father said.

' "Dear Parents," ' the son began. ' "Oh, mother, I am so lonely." It's all, all covered with blots same as if she were crying on the paper. "Daddy, why did I . . . why did I ever . . . ever . . ." it's hard to make it out . . . yes . . . "why did I ever come to this awful place? Say a prayer for me every night, mother. Kiss baby for me. Forgive me, mother. Your loving daughter Mary." '

When he finished there was utter silence for a long time. The father was the first to move. He rose slowly, still holding the cheque in his hand. Then he said:

'There was no word about the money in the letter,' he said in a queer voice. 'Why is that now?'

'Twenty pounds,' the mother said in a hollow voice. 'It isn't earned in a week.'

She snatched the letter furtively from her son and hid it ravenously in her bosom.

The father walked away slowly by the fence, whispering to himself in a dry voice:

'Aye! My greed stopped me asking myself that question. Twenty pounds.'

He walked away erect and stiff, like a man angrily drunk.

The others continued to sit about in silence, brooding. They no longer heard the larks. Suddenly one looked up and said in a frightened voice:

'What is father doing?'

They all looked. The father had passed out of the field into another uplying craggy field. He was now standing on a rock with his arms folded and his bare head fallen forward on his chest, perfectly motionless. His back was towards them but they knew he was crying. He had stood that way, apart, the year before, on the day their horse died.

Then the eldest son muttered a curse and jumped to his feet. He stood still with his teeth set and his wild eyes flashing. The infant boy dropped a weed from his tiny hands and burst into frenzied weeping.

Then the mother clutched the child in her arms and cried out in a despairing voice:

'Oh! Birds, birds, why do ye go on singing when my heart is frozen with grief.'

Together, they all burst into a loud despairing wail and the harsh sound of their weeping rose into the sky from the field that had suddenly become ugly and lonely; up, up into the clear blue sky where the larks still sang their triumphant melody.

A YOUNG bull was grazing in a green field above the village.

It was a beautiful summer morning. The grass was delicious, as the sun had scarcely dried the dew on it. The grass blades gleamed and they were moist. A faint smoke rose from the earth, and among the bushes of the fence there were filmy webs, like shining curtains of pale silk. Everywhere there were intoxicating sounds of life – the mumbling of insects, the whirring of bees, the warbling of birds. Little clouds of mist ascended into the sky, and away up in the emptiness, where the sun was shining beyond the brown peaks of the far-off hills, there were dazzling golden and white clouds in dizzy banks, like the gates of Paradise.

The young bull ate furiously of the luscious, dewy grass until he was sated. Then he began to march around the field, swinging his short tail and butting the air with his young horns. He was only a year old and was still almost unconscious of his sex; but this morning, for the first time, he felt a strange intoxication, caused by the wild, sensuous smells of nature and by the rich food he had eaten. He felt a desire for company and for violent exertion. He felt a tingling sensation under his hide, and his legs seemed to rise of their own accord and to strike the earth with unnecessary violence. His eyes grew moist. There was a rush of blood to his head, and like a half-drunken man he felt incapable of restraining a wild bellow. But as he did not know yet how to bellow properly, he merely made a faint mowing sound in his throat and his jaws slavered like a hungry calf.

Then he suddenly felt jolly and he began to trot around after his shadow, making rushes at it and butting the earth with his forehead.

There was a pump in the far corner of the field, about fifty yards from the fence. There was a path in the grass from the wooden gate in the fence to the pump. Beyond the gate a little narrow road led down the slope to the village. Village people came to the pump for water. The young bull was always interested and amused by the people who came to the pump for water. He used to stand at a distance from them and shoot out from his moist nostrils long columns of breath with a snuffling sound. It broke the monotony of the day watching these people come and go and listening to the rasping sound they made with the pump handle.

He strolled down towards the pump in the hope of seeing somebody.

Just then a little boy arrived at the wooden gate

carrying a bucket and a tin dipper. The little boy was whistling. When the bull saw the little boy he felt a curious sensation of melancholy and a desire to do something violent. So he bellowed and scraped the ground with his foot. The little boy closed the gate and then stood still, looking at the bull. The bull stood between him and the pump. The boy shouted. The bull tossed his head. The boy advanced a few paces, walking very erect. The bull began to tremble, and made rumbling noises in his throat. His body became rigid and his head grew dizzy with tension. The boy shouted again and advanced another step. He began to rattle the dipper against the bucket to terrify the bull. The sound excited the bull and he dashed forward with lowered head. His short tail stood out, rippling, with its little fringe of long hairs dangling.

The boy uttered a cry of fright and fled from the field, banging the gate after him. The bull swerved at the gate and then cantered about, making figures of eight, leaping and tossing his head. He felt delighted with the terror he had inspired in the little boy. He no longer felt fierce, but he felt that this was a splendid new game and that he would henceforth chase everybody that came into the field. So, in his joy, he went up to the pump and began to hammer it with his forehead.

After a few minutes he heard voices approaching the gate. He looked up. Two little boys were coming along the narrow road towards the gate. Their heads bobbed up and down between the gleaming wet tops of the bushes.

The little boy who had fled was now returning accompanied by another boy who was slightly bigger. The second boy was talking arrogantly and making gestures. He had something white under his jacket.

As they entered the gate the bull trotted towards them slowly, making a rumbling sound. Then he halted suddenly and snorted, as he caught sight of the white thing that was wriggling and whining under the jacket of the bigger boy. The boy lowered the white thing to the ground and took it by the ears. It was a tiny white dog with black spots on its ears. It was so small that when it stood on the ground the grass reached to its chest. Its legs were like spindles and its tail was long and thin like the tail of a rat. The bull smelt it even at that distance and it had a disgusting smell. He felt an extraordinary sensation of fear and repulsion.

Then the boy began to shake the little dog, holding him by the ears and shouting. The other little boy kept pointing to the bull and saying something in a loud shrill voice. The dog began to yelp on a high note. He bared his teeth and scraped the earth with his hind legs, trying to break loose. Then the boy let him go, and the little dog rushed forward.

He was so small and weak that he stumbled over the wet grass and fell head over heels with the first rush. Then he got up, barked shrilly, and looked back at the boys, with his right forefoot raised. The boys threatened him with their raised fists and urged him on. He ran forward towards the bull, biting at blades of grass, stopping to lick his wet legs and looking back at the boys with suspicion in his eyes. When he got near the bull the hair stood up on his neck, he put his tail between his legs, and he curved his back like a cat.

The bull had watched him with amazement as he approached. He stood perfectly still, with his head lowered and his flanks quivering. The approaching dog, so small that he could hardly see him crawling through the grass, inspired him with extraordinary terror. He didn't know what to make of the curious little white thing with the queer smell. He felt a desire to take to flight. When the dog stood still, however, with his tail between his legs, the bull could contain himself no longer and he rushed forward bellowing. The tiny dog jumped into the air and he began to yelp savagely. As the bull came upon him he turned and snapped his jaws, grazing the bull's snout.

Then indeed the bull succumbed to his terror. Throwing his head in the air, he bellowed loudly and took to flight. Snorting, with his tail in the air, he galloped away up the field, tearing up the grass with his flying hoofs. He disappeared over the brow of a mound into a hollow with a drifting column of his breath pursuing him.

Then the tiny dog became arrogant and fierce. He trotted after the fleeing bull slowly, barking, and snapping at imaginary flies. Now and again he looked behind at the cheering boys. Then again he would trot forward, with his foreleg bandied out and his tail raised aloft in a curl.

THE stream flowed from beneath a grey cliff, in which birds were twittering. Long ago, nobody now remembered when, they had made a stone passage for it down the short slope. Now the slope was covered with grass and briars. Where the stream emerged into the flat field below the village they had built a low stone wall, overarching, in a half-circle. Nobody in the village knew when it was built or who built it. Ancestors of the people built it; people whose bones were now sand, maybe, on the sea-shore. The stones of the wall were small with hoary age. No one touched them. Scorched moss covered them.

The stream emerged through a narrow crevice in a thin layer of black slate that passed beneath the black mould of the upper earth. It made a tiny white fountain before it fell into a small cup-shaped well in the limestone rock. It shone like silver, that cup in the rock, polished by the countless dippers that had scooped the precious water from it through the centuries.

From the well a spout of stone carried the over-flowing water into a muddy pool, in which cresses floated, growing, spreading out their spiced green branches.

The murmur of the ancient stream could be heard among the thatched houses of the village up above on the barren hill. Nature was utterly silent on that sultry summer day.

On a stone by the cup-shaped well a young woman sat, drawing water. She scooped out the water with a ringing sound until the cup was empty. Then she waited until it filled again from the white fountain. As she waited, she watched her little child, who played in the pool, wading among the cresses. She smiled happily, watching him.

Then she started and crossed herself. A shrivelled hag approached along the grassy path from the village. She leaned on a stick and mumbled to herself. She was almost double. Her red frieze petticoat touched the ground. Her head was hooded with a black shawl that was tied under her chin. Two fierce old eyes peered from beneath the peeked shawl malignantly. Her white lips were open, showing jagged teeth. The hand holding the stick was a great lean humpy bone, like the hip of an old horse. Her feet were bare. They were red and swollen, with enormous great-toes.

As the hag approached, the young woman arose hurriedly although her pail was but half full. She took her child by the hand and walked away, just as the hag entered the half-circle of the old stone wall.

Seeing the child, the hag grinned malignantly and tried to straighten herself.

'God between us and the Evil One,' the young woman cried, almost in a scream.

She hurried away with long strides. The hag looked after her, cackling with a mumbling sound, like the death rattle in a dying man's throat. Then she turned to the well and sat heavily on the stone. She struck the rock with her stick and murmured:

'Flow on, white water. Wash out his bones that are lost and play music for his spirit. Let nothing that is young be merry while you flow. Let blight fall on young bones and withering diseases fall on young brides that lie in the arms of their lovers.'

Then she bent low over her doubled knees and listened to the flowing white water. She listened to its mocking sound. Ancient and withered like the shrunken stones, sour like the floating cresses, a sapless thing without fertility, she listened to the murmur of the ancient stream that was still young. There it flowed, white and fresh, into its cup of silvered stone. She listened brooding. Her mind wandered back. She shivered and a strange light came into her demented eyes.

She saw the constant vision of her insanity.

A tall, slim maiden with dark hair and voluptuous lips. That was she. By this stream she met him on a summer evening. He had come to drink and there they kissed and pledged their troth. That was sixty years ago.

For a month she longed for him, her young body wild with shy desire. He and his brother shared out their father's land. Together they built a new house for the young bride. Then she married him. For two nights she shared his bed in ecstasy.

Then on the third evening, just after nightfall, his brother came. It was a summer night. The door was open and no light was lit. They were sitting by the fire after supper thinking of their bed.

Saluting, the brother entered and said:

'We are going to take birds' eggs at the salt cliff. Will you come with us, John?'

Her husband looked at her and smiled.

'Don't go,' she said.

His brother taunted him, saying:

'Marriage should not make you lose your manliness.'

Then he arose to go. She clung to him and begged him to stay with her. But he thrust her from him angrily, for his brother had taunted his manhood.

'There is no man born,' he said, 'who ever saw me afraid of a cliff.'

Then he took ropes and a sack and went away to the cliff with other young men of the village.

For a long time she sat alone by the dying fire after they had gone. The moon rose and cast its wan light on her doorway. Then she grew afraid. A torpor overspread her body and her mind filled with terrible visions that brought cold sweat to her brow. And she sat unable to move by the dead fire, watching the enchanted moonlight.

Suddenly the silent night became wild with imaginary sound. She sprang to her feet, uttering a wild shriek. Unaware that she herself had uttered it, she heard it, reverberating in her husband's voice, in the chaos into which her disordered mind had hurled the world. She saw the wild cliff with death astride its belly.

With the shriek still ringing in her ears, she dashed from the house. The village was abed, as she passed, flying, through the silent street. The moonlit thatch and the weird stones watched her like spectres. Soon she heard the murmur of the sea and she saw its bosom, lit by the moon; a glittering stream of yellow light, stretching afar through a dark, heaving plain.

She went along the summits of the silent cliffs. And still she heard the ringing shriek. At last she saw a group of men ahead of her. She paused. Her body became rigid. They were gesticulating. They were shouting too; but although she heard their words she did not understand. Their words were meaningless.

With a gasp she ran forward. They caught her in their arms and dragged her back from the cliff's edge. Her eyes were fixed and she bit their hands. They tied her with a rope. Then she became silent and lay still.

Now she suffered no pain and she no longer heard the shriek. Her body was numb and her mind was tired, as if it had become a heavy cloud that had no feeling. Yet she knew that he alone was absent. And she saw his death in their eyes. She saw a rope tethered to a heavy stone. She saw its other end too, torn. Men were fingering it with horror in their eyes. They had pulled it up that way, with a torn end.

Suddenly his brother shouted in a frenzy:

'We killed him, pulling at the knot when it got entangled in the cliff.'

'Hush,' said another. 'She hears you.'

'Let her,' he said. 'What is there for her but the tomb.'

'Aye,' they said. 'Or worse. Long grief.

'Get me ready now,' said his brother. 'I'm going down for him.'

So she heard them speak, but she made no movement and she felt no pain. She watched them with childish curiosity.

Then they put a rope around his brother. He blessed himself and they lowered him down the face of the cliff. He had a sack tied to his arm. As he disappeared over the cliff, she saw his face cold and fierce. He was brave too like her man, his brother.

As they waited, a man soothed her with words, but she made no answer. Then she saw them haul the rope. They raised it carefully over the cliff's edge. The sack was bulging. Her face became white and she began to giggle foolishly.

'She is mad,' they whispered.

Again they lowered the rope and hauled up his brother. The brother's face was still bold and fearless but very white.

'He was not all there,' he said with set teeth. 'The tide had carried off his head and his legs.'

The brother's arms and hands were bloody.

They carried her home between them. She kept asking them childishly:

'What have ye got in that sack?'

Then sixty years passed. All those years she never wept. Her sorrow grew like a cancer; so powerfully, that even death could not snatch her. No other lover dared to look into her fearful eyes. Her body withered until it was like her soul. She became a thing of horror to the village. When she passed anything young she spat and cursed.

And always she came each day to the stream where he had first kissed her.

The vision exhausted itself. The hag's eyes grew tired. Her ugly lips curled. She looked again into the silver bowl of stone and struck the rock with her stick.

'Flow on, white water,' she muttered. 'Flow over his lost bones. You crooning witch, you have seen them all die. They all die and you flow on, you little witch.'

So she spoke, sitting by the mocking stream.

Aт dawn, on a wild October morning, a red-bearded rider came from the mountains into the seaside village of Carrig. He came looking for a priest. At the parochial house he said in a loud voice that a man in the hamlet of Prochlais was on the point of death from an unknown disease. The doctor was away, he said, and the district nurse declared that it was neither typhus nor scarlet fever nor any kind of pock known to her, and that a priest should be brought. The sick man's name was Lydon. He was a strong young man five days ago. Now he was moaning on his belly, refusing food and drink.

When the parish priest was awakened from his sleep, he growled and told his housekeeper to send the rider to the curate's house. So the curate was roused and mounted on the white mare that the rider had brought from the mountains.

'The wind'll be in yer back,' roared the man with the red beard to the curate, 'so you best go straight over Cockrae and then down over the Devil's Pass into our village. She's a good mare, only whip her on her right flank, never on her left.'

The curate galloped away on the white mare. Then the man with the red beard roused the tavern keeper. Shaking the rain out of his long beard, he stood on the floor and told everybody in a loud and furious voice that a strange disease had stricken a young man in his village; a strong young man called Lydon, who was now lying on his belly, moaning and refusing food and drink. He said it was a strange disease the man had and that the people were afraid of it.

The curate lashed his horse up the mountain road, grumbling at the unseemly hour and the rain and the storm that was cutting into his back from the sea behind. He was approaching middle age, but although he had been twenty years wandering around the wild district from parish to parish, he was still terrified of the people and considered them to be no whit more civilized than wild men of the African forests. Especially the natives of Prochlais where he was going. And this strange new disease?

'What on earth can it be now?' he thought.

The rain pattered on his black waterproof cape and on his felt hat that was slouching about his ears. He shuddered with fear, both of the fury of nature and of the strange disease he was going to encounter in the barbarous hamlet among the mountains.

When the ascending road grew steeper, the white mare broke from a gallop into that crouching trot which is peculiar to mountain horses. She moved as if dragging a heavy weight, with her hind legs spread and her neck stretched, scattering loose stones from the rough road with her scrambling hoofs. Here there were overhanging trees and the wind died down behind the shoulder of a hill. The rain fell heavier with a soft, mournful, thudding sound. Sodden leaves floated down from the tree branches and an odd bird, breaking from its shelter, fluttered on ragged wet wings farther into the woods. Streams of water, reddened by the granite soil, gurgled through the cavities of the road and splashed against the mare's white flanks and against the black coat of the priest. They passed the trees, on through a rocky gorge, past a herd's cottage and then came to a wide moor covered with heather and black bog. The sky sank low about them. The horizon became a sloping bank of sagging mist, quite close. The rain poured down aslant, driven by a furious whistling wind.

The curate was drenched to the bone. He grew furious with the strange disease that had befallen the unknown man in that weird hamlet that was an eyesore on God's earth. And why should he be dragged out at dawn, drenched with rain and frozen to the marrow by a cruel wind for this unnecessary, savage man, who had contracted a strange disease? The ghostly, desolate place became full of spooks and witch devils in his imagination. He lashed the mare furiously.

Goaded by the stinging whip, the dripping mare

stretched out into a fierce gallop along the dull sounding bog road, up a steep ascent into the narrow gullet of the Devil's Pass. Here the shaggy rocks rose frowning like macabre statues with drooping heads, in zigzag rows, and the narrow road wound among them, descending slowly, until it debouched precipitously into a gloomy valley that was walled with great round mountains. Through the rain and clouds of mist the hamlet of Prochlais became visible at the bottom of the valley, a desolate, grey place, huddled among rocks and willow trees, by the bank of a stream that wandered through marsh-land. The mare neighed when she saw it, and flew into a head-long pace, scarcely touching the road. The curate hung on grimly, with his hands grasping her mane and his coat about his ears.

They halted in the village street. The village people crowded around, shouting to one another. They helped the priest to dismount. He looked around at them, frowning.

He only knew them very slightly, as the priests of the parish avoided this village as much as possible. They said nothing could be done for these people. They were full of superstition, wild, untamable people, incapable of understanding the subtleties of the Christian faith, by profession sheep stealers. But as they stole sheep from one another they did not profit very much by that trade. Walled in by their mountains as in a prison, intermarriage had bred lunacy and decadence amongst them. Their houses were hovels. It was impossible to get any of them to pay their clerical dues, yet they were always begging at the parochial house.

That was the opinion held of them by the priests and in particular by the curate, who secretly loathed them and considered them entirely unnecessary human beings, although from the altar he was forced to admit that they were of value in the hereafter because of their immortal souls.

At this moment, as he stood among them, drenched to the skin and numb with the cold, still fasting, he wished that the ground would open up and swallow the wretches; especially the one who had the strange disease.

'Where is the man who has the strange disease?' he cried angrily.

The people had been babbling until he spoke. Then their joy at seeing a stranger gave way to their fear of the strange disease that had appeared among them. They became silent. A woman came forward, curtsied and said that she was the sick man's mother. Walking sideways, through courtesy, she led the priest to an old thatched hovel, that had no window in its front wall. Smoke was coming out the doorway.

Then she stepped aside, curtsied with queenly grace and begged the priest 'to honour her humble hut by blessing it with his sacred presence.' The priest entered the kitchen. She followed him. The whole village crowded around the door.

At first the curate could see nothing in the room. On the hearth there was a turf fire, which emitted an extraordinary quantity of smoke without making any blaze. The smoke did not go up the chimney, as they probably had not cleaned it for years. So that the kitchen was dense with smoke. The curate began to cough and his eyes became rheumy. That aggravated his rage.

'Have you no light?' he said.

The woman fetched a candle, stuck it into the fire and brought it forth flickering, covered with yellow ashes and melting tallow. She held the disreputable candle over her head and pointed to a corner of the room.

'There he is, father,' she said.

The priest went to the corner and looked down. On the earthen floor there was a rough straw mattress. A young man, fully dressed, lay, face downwards, on the mattress.

'Is this the sick man?' said the priest.

'Yes, father,' said the woman.

The priest took the candle and put it on the rough

chair that had been placed beside the mattress. He stooped down and touched the recumbent figure.

'Is he asleep?' he said.

'No, father,' murmured the sick man in a mournful, but very strong voice.

'Ha,' said the priest angrily, standing up suddenly. 'You don't speak like a sick man.'

The sick man sat up and looked at the priest. His face was close to the flickering candle. It stood out, deadly pale and frenzied, with large blue eyes and thick lips. He wore a blue jersey that left his powerful neck exposed. He had a magnificent neck, rising like a pyramid to a skull that was also beautiful. His foolish features, pale and decadent, looked sacrilegious, facing such a glorious pedestal. His limbs and frame loomed large and soft in the gloom.

'Tell them to leave the room, father,' he said in a whining voice. 'I want to speak to ye.'

'Clear out, all of you,' said the priest.

'Well?' he continued, when everybody had gone.

There was an awkward silence. The sick man was trying to say something, but although his lips moved, no sound came from them. He passed a large soft hand back and forth over his closely shorn skull irresolutely.

'Let's see,' said the curate irritably. 'What's your name?'

'Patrick Lydon, father.'

'How old are you?'

'Twenty-two, father.'

'Ha! And . . . have you a pain? Come on, man, speak up.'

'Uh . . . uh . . .' stammered the man. 'Father, will ye put out the candle?'

'What?'

'I'm ashamed to tell ye, father,' cried the fellow in a loud, trembling voice. 'But if ye put out the candle it 'u'd be easier to tell ye in the dark. I'm ashamed o' me life.'

'What on earth . . .?'

'Ah, father. . . .'

'All right, all right, I'll put it out.'

The priest quenched the candle. The sick man seized the candle with his trembling hand and took it off the chair.

'Would ye sit down, father?' he blubbered. 'It 'u'd be easier for me to tell ye if ye were sittin' down beside me. I'm ashamed o' me life.'

'Eh?' said the priest.

He sat down.

'Go ahead now,' he said.

The man clutched the priest's knee and began to weep aloud.

'Oh! father,' he said, 'I'm ashamed o' me life. I . . . I . . .'

'What?'

'I . . . I . . . I . . .'

'Speak, you fool. What is it?'

'I . . . I . . . I'm in lo—o—o—ve, father.'

He threw himself on the mattress and began to moan.

'What?' gasped the priest. 'Eh? You . . . you . . . My God! I'll . . . I'll . . .'

'Don't curse me, father,' said the man, springing up again. 'It's Nora Tierney, father, I'm in love with, the blacksmith's wife, and I'm afraid to look at her; but her face does be beckoning to me and I can't swallow me breath. Anoint me, father, 'cos I want to die. But don't curse me.'

The priest stood up, made a noise with his lips and then raised his hands to his face. His rage burst forth. He thought of the ride through the blinding rain and the wind, and the misery of life tending on such wretches. He rushed to the door.

'Hand me that whip,' he yelled.

They brought him the whip. The sick man began to scream.

'Don't curse me, father,' he cried.

The priest began to lash him furiously. Then the lout jumped up and ran to the door, uttering piercing yells, which were lusty with vigorous health. He ran down the village street and vaulted a stone fence into the bog. He kept on running, yelling all the while.

'Glory be to God,' said somebody, 'he's cured. What ailed him at all?'

'Eh?' said the priest, brandishing his whip. 'Bring me my horse.'

The villagers gaped in silence, terrified, as he mounted his horse and rode away. No one dared speak to him, to inquire what had happened.

Riding slowly up the mountain road, the priest kept shuddering with cold and anger. Tears of indignation and hopeless misery came into his eyes. The hopelessness of trying to vent his anger on the idiotic villagers made him want to cry like a child.

Then at last he drew in a deep breath, dilated his eyes and turned his wrath on the devil, who was the cause of the whole thing. He threatened the sagging clouds with his clenched fist and cried out aloud:

'This disgusting . . . this DEGRADING passion of love.'

O N a summer afternoon an old man was walking
along the narrow stony road that led from his
village to the sea. One hand supported his hip. In
the other he gripped a stick upon which he leaned
heavily. His laboured breath made a singing sound.
At every third or fourth step he halted, straightened
himself slowly, grasped his stick with both hands
and looked about him, with the brooding, melancholy expression of an aged man on his withered face.

His body had shrunk. His clothes hung loose upon him. They were covered with patches. He wore
only garments that had been discarded as useless
by the young men of the house. For he had become
useless and a burden. Although it was hot, he wore
numbers of garments. Yet he did not perspire
and he was buttoned tightly. There was no heat
in his blood. His face was yellow. His eyes were
colourless. They were bloody around the rims. They
had no lashes. His toothless mouth had sunk into
his face. His cheek-bones stuck out beneath the taut
skin like the hip bones of an old horse. On his
twisted hands the skin was transparent, showing a
web of sickly veins beneath. A thin white beard
grew on his neck beneath his chin. Although it was
dead calm, his tattered black hat was secured with a

cord, tied around his neck, after the manner of a fisherman at sea.

When he walked, his ferruled stick made a queer, plaintive sound on the polished limestone flags of the road and on the loose stones that lay there. His feet fell heavily, unsteadily, slipping and crunching, like the hoofs of a heavily-laden horse, stumbling at night through a rocky mountain pass.

There was no sound anywhere. Everything was still. The sea was so calm that its murmur did not reach him even though it lay but five hundred yards away, glassy and white in the sunlight. On either side of the path there were little green gardens of oats and potatoes. He often leaned over their stone fences and blessed the growing crops and looked for labourers and was glad when he saw none; for it was unlucky for a fisherman to meet people on his way to the sea.

The old man was doting. He had the mirage of returned youth in his brain. He thought he was going to sea as of yore.

He reached the end of the path and crawled through a style that led into a wide craggy stretch of waste land above the shore. Now he could smell the odour of brine and a faint thrill of joy passed through his body. He stood erect, shielded his eyes and looked ahead. He saw the vast expanse of level, glittering water stretching to the confines of the sky before him. He saw the long mound of boulders on the shore. He saw the upturned coracles on the flags among the boulders on the shore, their tarred bottoms gleaming in the sunlight. He saw the cliffs rising on either side of the rocky cove and the silent sea, swelling up and falling down around the black rocks. He saw the cocks of dried seaweed and patches of seamoss, being bleached white, spread out, gathered that morning by the village women. And all the joyous memories of boyhood came to him in a wild shower that sent his remaining blood coursing passionately through his veins.

He went forward, moving his lips, trembling, now almost moving quickly and vigorously, for the mirage had become so vivid that he thought himself waking from a long sleep and entering the land of youth. And he was going forth to fish.

As he came near the mound of boulders, he heard the ponderous lapping of the waves, tumbling slowly without foam, about the rocks, and the smell of the sea became so strong that it was like food entering his lungs. He took his hand from his hip and swung it unsteadily, by his side. His stick struck the path fiercely. His eyes gleamed.

Overcome by this joy, he rested on a stone bench by the side of the path. This stone bench had been built there, ages ago, by the fishermen, for resting their baskets of fish, on their way from the shore to the village. Resting there also brought wonderful memories to his mind. And he thought of his first great catch of fish as a young man, when there was soft down on his unshaven face. He remembered resting his full basket there and looking at the soft dead fish, with their slime hardened into a jelly. How wonderful that was!

And then suddenly he remembered the stone. And as he remembered it he stopped breathing and slowly turned about and leaned his chest against the bench and examined the rocky ground looking for it. He saw it and started eagerly, like a hunting dog catching sight of its prey. It was a round block of granite. It sparkled as the sunshine shone on the particles of mica in its surface. It lay on the ground, on a clear space between the rocks. All round it there were bruised stones, bruised to a powder and where it lay there was a little hollow.

That stone had lain in that place as long as the oldest traditions in the village could remember. And from time immemorial it had been the custom of the young men of the village to test their strength by lifting it. It was a great day in each young man's life when he raised the stone from the ground and 'gave it wind,' as they said. And if he raised it to his knees, he was a champion, the equal of the best. And if he raised it to his chest he was a hero, a phenomenon of strength and men talked of him. Whereas, he who failed to lift it from the ground became the butt of everybody's scorn. It had always been so, from the time of the most remote ancestors of the people.

The old man looking at it became very fierce, as he remembered the first time he had lifted it. He was barely seventeen and he came secretly after night-fall and tussled with it, until every muscle in his body ached. But he had lifted it, just an inch. No more. And little by little, he had raised it higher, until he began to be spoken of with respect, by the young men and old who came there on Sundays, during the trials of strength.

Then he recalled the great triumph of his life, and his bleary eyes filled with tears so that he could not see the stone at which he peered. But he saw it in his mind vividly, in the grey dawn, slippery with dew. There had been a wedding in the village. The youths of the district were gathered, numbering among them many men who were famous for their strength and beauty. All night they made merry, and then when daylight was streaming through the open door of the crowded house, somebody challenged them in a loud voice to put their boasting to the test and to go over to the shore and see who would lift the granite stone highest on his body. Shouting and laughing they set forth, followed by many women. And there they stripped themselves and rubbed their muscles and seized upon the stone. But he alone of all those strong men raised it to his throat and kissed it with his lips, three times, before he dropped it between his wide-spread legs on its bed of powdered stones. And the shout that was raised that day before sunrise by the people of his village now rang as loudly in his ears as if it still floated on the air.

Mumbling, he left the bench and, throwing away his stick, he went stooping to the stone. He staggered heavily without his stick, but he was unaware of what he was doing. His eyes were fixed and they gleamed with the light of madness. He reached the stone, steadied himself and stood erect, looking down upon it. Then he raised his hands to his mouth, spat into his palms and rubbed them together. He blew out a great breath and shook himself. Then he began to scratch the ground with his feet, getting a foothold. He set his legs wide apart, slightly bending forward at the knees. His body was trembling violently, but he did not notice it. Then he stooped over the stone.

First he placed his hands upon it and then paused, breathing slowly. His breath whistled with asthma

239

and it came out irregularly, in gulps. Then he began to move his palms over the stone, slowly, seeking a grip. Its surface was so round that it was impossible to get a grip anywhere except by encircling its bulk with the arms. So he bent lower and reached down with his hands. But his body had become so shrunken with old age that his arms could not cover sufficient of its bulk to enable him to get a grip. And he twisted about, growling and pawing at it, enraged at the impotence of his arms. His knees bent more and more. He began to groan. Then he knelt before it and stooped until he was touching it with his chest. He spread out his arms over it. His hands touched the ground. Then he could at last grip the stone. He pressed and then became still. The effort had exhausted his lungs. His tongue was sticking out. He panted for breath. His eyes began to become covered with a glaze.

Then he began to feel the stone against his body. It had become hot under the blazing sun. It had an exciting, maddening effect on him. A big red blotch came before his eyes. His body stiffened and a lump, like a knot, came into his throat. His blood rushed to his head. The veins on his forehead became big. He sucked in his lips, groaned, drew in a great breath with a rattling sound and heaved at the stone. It remained absolutely motionless. He fell over it loosely, with his arms thrown out limply. His chin struck the stone. His back shivered. Then he stiffened, shook violently from head to foot and rolled off the stone, falling on his left side. His legs shot out. He tried to raise his head, but it dropped back over his left shoulder and remained that way, his face staring at the sky. His lower jaw dropped. A little yellow wisp of moisture oozed out over his lower lip. For a few moments his body shuddered and then he became terribly still, with his eyes wide open and his lower jaw hanging.

Flies began to buzz about him. Presently one settled on the yellow stream that was oozing from his mouth. Another came and the two flies quarrelled about his mouth, buzzing violently. He lay thus for a long time, motionless. There was dead silence except for the buzzing of the flies.

Then human voices broke the stillness. People appeared, coming from the village, calling and shielding their eyes, as they looked about, searching. They entered the craggy field where he lay and came on without seeing him until they were within ten yeards of his body. Then they shouted and came running to him. When they stooped over him, the two men took off their caps and crossed themselves and the women uttered a loud wail. The old man was dead.

A middle-aged man with grey hair, who was kneeling beside the corpse, said in a loud voice:

'We couldn't keep him indoors this last week. He kept stealing out. See? Trying to lift the stone he was. It broke his heart.'

He was the dead man's son.

The other man, a neighbour, said reverently:

'There was a day, then, when he could lift it high. Praised be God. There is nothing in all creation that isn't more lasting than man.'

They raised the corpse and carried it away on their clasped hands. A woman spat upon the stone and crossed herself.

'It's the devil of pride,' she said, 'that brought sin first into the world.'

Then they went away, talking loudly and lamenting.

Later, when evening came, people came to look at the stone out of curiosity, to see where the old man had died. And they talked of his youth and of his strength and of the wedding night when he kissed the stone three times, holding it level with his throat. And then, youths who were there challenged one another to a test of strength. They strippped themselves and began to tussle with the stone.

I N the village of Liosnamara there was a peasant
family called O'Toole. The village was beside the
sea. All the other inhabitants were fishermen, because all the land in the village was a barren rock
except the fifteen acres which O'Toole possessed.
Therefore the fishermen, who risked the danger of
the Atlantic, despised O'Toole as a landlubber; and
O'Toole, having land, despised the fishermen who
had none. On this account O'Toole and his family
were more or less at enmity with the rest of the
village.

This enmity was instinctive and not active in any
sense; because all the fishermen were at heart gentle
and simple people. O'Toole, on the contrary, was an
extraordinary, complex fellow.

They called him Red Michael in the village because of his reddish hair and beard. He was a lean,
little man, with a long, crooked nose, small grey eyes
that were always red at the corners and with deep
furrows in his forehead. He always looked old, even
when he was a young man. He was a silent fellow as
a rule and he preferred being alone to mixing with
the villagers. Even when he visited the broad flag
in front of the village, where the men conversed in
the evening, he stood in the rear, with his hands

clasped behind his back, leaning forward, craning his neck and listening suspiciously as if he expected something malicious to be said of him. They talked of fish, nets and the tides; whereas O'Toole was only interested in land. In this way he had no outlet for his thoughts. They considered him to be a mean, dour, avaricious man, the very demon for work.

Sometimes, however, he was seized with an irresistible desire to go on a drinking bout. He might be digging in a field when this desire came. If so, he hurled his spade to the ground. He rushed home. With violent oaths he demanded all the money in the house. He ransacked the cupboards until he found the money, because his wife hid the long, embroidered, folding, cloth money purse in unusual places. It there was no money, he took a few yards of frieze cloth or even a young pig to the shopkeeper at the postal village of Carra. He sold whatever he took for half its price. Then he began to drink.

As a rule the drinking bout lasted a week. During the week the dour, industrious, silent man became an abandoned libertine. He was garrulous. He fought. He visited the loose women of the district. He went about in a filthy condition. He begged money from the doctor, the curate and even from the magistrate. When all his money was spent he returned home. He went on his two knees to his wife

and begged her to beat him. If she refused he rolled
on the floor and wept. Then she beat him and he was
comforted. He returned to work and he seemed
quite normal until the time arrived for another bout.

His wife was also an unusual woman. She was of
a much finer type than her husband. She was in no
sense pretty, but she had a commanding figure, tall,
well built, with a powerful head. Her square sallow
face bore a strange resemblance to the face of a lion-
ess. She had large, brooding, menacing, blue eyes.
Her hair was black and each strand was strong and
stiff. Being a peasant's wife she kept at a distance
from the fishermen's wives. She hardly ever entered
into conversation with them, but went about 'with
her head in the air.' Possibly she was ashamed of
her husband's occasional depravity and in order to
hide her shame from the other women she kept aloof
from them. She really was a refined and sensitive
woman.

The village people thought she was a bit queer,
but they admired her. They thought her queer because she had a habit of looking out over the cliff
tops at the sea with her hands clasped on her bosom
like a man, standing motionless for an hour at a time.
They liked her for her generosity. She had a cow,
the only one in the village, and she gave the others
milk; free of course.

In the first years of their married life the O'Toole couple had two sons and a daughter. They were normal, healthy children, who gave no trouble to their parents and their parents did not take any particular interest in them, as is customary among peasants. The father continued his periodic drinking bouts and the mother stared at the sea. And then, when the youngest child was thirteen years old, another son was born. They called him Peter. Red Michael was then forty-four and Mary, his wife, was forty.

The event aroused considerable curiosity in the village. The men made fun of Red Michael, laughingly calling him a wicked old rascal. 'After thirteen years,' they said, 'who would expect it of you?' Instead of laughing with them, Red Michael became furiously angry. He vented his spleen on the baby. The other children were also teased by the village children. So they also grumbled at the unwelcome baby. Added to that, the baby was a weakling. It caused dreadful annoyance for many months by contracting every possible disease with which babies are cursed.

'I say, woman,' Red Michael bawled at his wife, 'you have given birth to a fairy child. There's a spell on him.'

'No,' said the wife, 'but he's a child of God. Pros-

246

perity will enter your house, Red Michael, with this son of mine.'

Strangely enough, the mother, who had been indifferent to her other children, was madly in love with this squalling mite. She often stayed up all night crooning to him. Red Michael was amazed and almost terrified, watching his hitherto sombre and silent wife becoming as playful as a young girl and as tender as a sheep towards the miserable little weakling. He became very melancholy. He ceased going on drinking bouts. He no longer visited the broad flag. He spent the evenings by his fireside, brooding in silence and watching his wife counting the little naked toes of the baby that sprawled on her lap.

'There's witchery in this,' he muttered.

For days at a time he never spoke a word to his family, or indeed to anybody.

But as the years passed his wife's prophecy came true. The family began to grow prosperous. Probably it was through his wife's efforts, because she became a very demon for thrift. She made everybody bustle. She nagged at her husband until she forced him to do various little jobbing contracts. She procured a position for her daughter Margaret as waitress at the hotel in the town, and a little later the second son, John, entered the service of the same hotel as a coachman. The eldest son, Joseph, became

a carpenter. And these three children were industrious, dutiful, temperate and intensely religious. The
mother drew every penny of their savings from them.
Every penny went into the long, embroidered, cloth
purse. But still the father grumbled. He grumbled
because his two sons had deserted the land of their
ancestors.

'What am I working for?' he cried. 'Who is to
come after me? Amn't I disgraced entirely, with one
fine son a common tradesman and the other making
a show of himself, driving every rascal in the town all
over the place? And isn't it a shame to have my
daughter slaving on a neighbour's floor? And will
ye tell me, Mary, what good will that weakling,
Peter, ever be, to tear up the fallow soil or build a
fence of heavy stones? Ach!'

'You fool!' answered his wife angrily. 'Do ye
think I'd let my children spend their lives in this
miserable village? Wasn't I lonely and sad here all
my life myself? And what good is your land? A few
rocks. No, Michael. I'll never let one of my children
be a slave same as I am. And as for my little Peter' —
here her voice became tender — 'he'll be the best of
them all. He'll be a clerk in the town and he'll come
home to his mother on a bicycle. Won't they all be
jealous when they see my little one coming home to
me on a bicycle like a gentleman?'

'Huh!' muttered Red Michael. 'Gentleman! Can a gentleman till the earth?'

And he would rush out of the house.

The villagers were already jealous of the prosperity which 'the child of God' had brought to the O'Toole family. They no longer despised Red Michael and they feared his wife. So they vented their spleen on little Peter, who had begun to toddle about. The other children threw mud at him and cried, 'See-i, see-i, you came late from the womb, you are crabbed.'

Little Peter, being delicate, was naturally inclined to be shy and morbid. The malice of the villagers made him still more gloomy. He had violent headaches and at night he had nightmares. But now and again he had fits of gaiety, during which he laughed boisterously, told his mother wonderful stories and played extraordinary pranks. His mother was delighted with these manifestations of abnormality, whereas they irritated the father. Often the village people saw the mother and son on a grassy knoll together; the mother with her black hair loose, singing; the son lying on his back at her feet.

Peter was sent to the village school. But for many years it was difficult to teach him anything. At school he proved to be obstinate and prone to violent tempers. In fact he became 'a regular young rake' as the schoolmaster said. And curiously enough, he grew strong and healthy during these years. So the other children, seeing he had become like themselves, stopped teasing him and made him their captain. Then, when Peter was ten years old, he underwent a marvellous change.

He came home from school one day and told his mother he wanted to be a bishop, and not 'a clerk.' 'Why little one?' said his mother.

'I want to wear a cloak made of gold,' said Peter, 'and a pointed cap and carry a big golden stick. Lovely.'

'Yes, but you'd have to be a priest first.'

'Then, I'll be a priest.'

'But you'll have to be good and pray hard and learn everything.'

'All right, mother, I will.'

'And it takes a lot of money to make a boy a priest.'

'All right, mother,' said Peter. 'I'll kill Timoney the publican and I'll take all his money, same as a pirate, when I get big.'

'Hush, hush,' said his mother, 'what things you say! All right, Peter. Maybe I'll get the money for you.'

Then Mrs. O'Toole's ambition swelled within her. Her son a priest! It was the highest ambition of a peasant. She consulted her husband. He growled, but still . . . 'there was no going against it. It was a big thing surely.' The other children were consulted. They were enthusiastic about it. It would reflect credit on them. And they were especially struck by the fact that Peter had become pious, industrious and showed marvellous intelligence at school.

'There ye are,' said his mother. 'The breath of God has fallen on him. He's a child of God. Children, we must save every penny to make him a priest. If I have to break stones on the road and sell my mother's wedding ring I'll do it.'

When he was twelve years old, Peter was sent to a small ecclesiastical seminary in the town. The faces of the villagers went green with jealousy.

For six years everything progressed favourably, until the unfortunate event, with which this story begins. Peter had a wonderful career at the seminary. His genius was the talk of the whole district. Year after year he came home laden with prizes. His mother was in an ecstasy of happiness. 'Before I die,' she would say, 'I'll confess my sins to my own son.' Even Red Michael had become resigned to 'the loss' of all his sons. He still mourned in his heart but he was gradually becoming impressed by his new social importance. He wore a swallow-tailed coat going to Mass on Sundays. He had his house slated and had a stove put into the kitchen instead of an open hearth. And the parish priest now called on him as a friend.

At the same time, however, money grew scarce in the house. The savings were entirely spent after four years. The other children all got married. Michael married a woman who kept a small shop in Carra; Joseph married the postmistress at Carra. Margaret married the police sergeant in the neighbouring village of Lisheen. Having families of their own, it was now difficult to get a penny from them. But the mother was so excited by the glorious future that she paid no heed to this. She borrowed money everywhere. The family fell into debt.

Then the disaster came like a thunderbolt. It was simply a letter from the president of the seminary announcing that Peter had been expelled. There were no explanations. The father and mother were both stupified. For three days they were quite incapable of even making enquiries. No news came from Peter himself. Then at last Red Michael called in his children. There was an uproar in the house. The violence with which the married children hurled abuse at Peter was extraordinary. Then they turned on the old people. 'Their' money had been squandered. 'Their' good name was dragged in the gutter. The 'shame of it' would drive 'them' out of the district. The mother was inarticulate and, strange to say, it was Red Michael who defended his son.

'Shut up,' he cried, 'and get out of my house. I'm

glad he's expelled. What do I want with a priest? I want a son to till my land and come after me. This place is his whenever he likes to come back for it.'

'Not likely,' cried Margaret, a stout woman of thirty. 'You owe us money and the land will have to be divided among us. He'll never get a sod of it.'

'Get out of my house,' cried the old man.

Nothing happened for a year. The mother reverted to her old habits of staring at the sea and going about with her head in the air. Of course 'the shame' leaked out even though the family tried to keep it a secret. But nobody could learn the cause of the expulsion, even though the inquisitive parish priest made a special journey to the town in order to ferret out the secret. Peter had disappeared. The village people now pitied the O'Tooles and they treated them very kindly indeed, since they had no longer any cause of jealousy. The poor old couple were indeed in a lonely and miserable condition, trying to meet the overdue bills that came pouring in, as soon as their 'shame' became known.

Then suddenly, after a year, Peter arrived home one evening. It was a night in April. The lamps had just been lit in the village. Everything was silent, except the sea that murmured softly in the distance, thudding mournfully against the bases of the cliffs. The soft, cool April night seemed to be listening to this distant thudding sound and the people sat in their cabins, listening, rocked peacefully by the sound of the sea.

Thus, when Peter suddenly lifted the latch and walked into the kitchen of his home, he found his parents sitting by the fireside in silence, brooding sorrowfully, as if they were listening to the murmur of the distant sea.

'Jesus, Mary and Joseph,' his mother cried, staring at him.

The father did not speak, but he rose to his feet slowly. His queer old face assumed a ludicrous expression of joy. Then he wiped his gnarled hand on his trousers and held it out to his son.

Peter came forward with tears in his eyes. He shook hands with his father in silence. Father and son looked one another in the eyes for a moment, softly, tenderly. The father muttered something and then pointed with his eyes towards the mother. Immediately Peter threw himself on his knees at her feet. Sobbing they embraced wildly. She took his head in her hands and covered him with kisses. Then she touched his limbs with her hands, uttering little cries of joy. The father watched them trembling. He also wept. For a long time not a word was spoken and their sobbing was so gentle that, above it, the distant murmur of the sea could be heard.

At last they grew calm and a tense embarrassment followed the outburst of joy. Peter murmured something about his driver being outside on the road. He went out with his father and after a little while returned with a trunk. The mother had put the kettle on the stove. She laid the table in the kitchen for tea. Yet it seemed they could talk of nothing but the weather. They spoke in snatches, but the old couple furtively examined Peter, and Peter in turn cast hasty and searching glances at the old couple.

A great change had come over the old people since Peter had seen them last. It seemed that decrepitude had swooped down upon them. The mother's hair was still dark and her strong sallow face had not wrinkled. But there was a weary look in her eyes and her gait was slow and uncertain. The father's hair had gone quite grey. All his teeth had gone and his cheeks had fallen in. Yet his body was still as hardy as ever. It seemed that the natural apathy of his mind had not been affected as much by the 'shame' as the mind of his sensitive wife had been.

Peter had undergone an extraordinary change. Even though he was only nineteen he had matured. He was very thin, but there was resolution in his deep grey eyes and the pale skin of his cheeks was smooth and flawless. His voluptuous lips were firmly set. His fair hair was shorn closely. He wore a close fit-

ting blue suit, rather smart, with a very light blue
shirt and collar and a black bow tie. His body was
symmetrically built and his limbs filled his clothes
elegantly. Sitting with his elbows on his knees, he
looked perfectly at ease, a dominant fellow, full of
vitality. The old people were very nervous looking
at him. They could hardly recognize him as their
son, their brooding son who sometimes laughed boisterously, but who was like themselves. Whereas this
MAN had some strange force in him, entirely alien
to their natures.

At last Peter broke the silence, for it was a silence,
since they merely uttered commonplaces, totally irre-
levant to the questions that troubled their minds.

'I suppose you are wondering what happened,' he
said.

The mother was going to the table with a jug
when he spoke. She halted suddenly and looked at
him furtively. Then she hastily placed the jug on the
table, wiped her hands in her apron and sat down in
front of the fire. The father opened his lips and
looked at her, terrified.

'Yes, we were wondering,' said the mother. Then
suddenly she burst into a flood of tears, silently and
weeping silently she murmured: 'But now you are
back to us what does it matter? Now everything is
done and . . .'

'Yes,' cried the father furiously, 'what does it matter? Now you are back. This place is yours. No man can raise a hand to you.'

It is unexplainable. But the two of them felt in their minds that this strange being, who had been their son, was so utterly remote from them that they were terrified of hearing anything of his past. It is impossible to explain the instinct of peasants, their aversion for anything unlike themselves and their intuition for sensing the presence in strangers of forces which are alien to their own natures.

But Peter felt none of this. He looked at them in astonishment. Then something struck him in the chest suddenly. He felt an aching pain, not in his heart, but in his lungs, as if he were short of breath. His eyes opened wide. He saw the strange look of fear on the faces of his parents. Then he too became afraid, for extraordinary and shameful thoughts struggled into his mind. Had he not longed to come back? Had he not longed for hours in distant, distant London, to see these beloved faces once more, to touch these toil-worn hands, to hear these voices, of which he knew every delicate intonation, to kiss those lips that murmured when he kissed them, maternal lips that crooned to him as a child? Had his eyes not grown moist and his body loosened with a delicious agony of longing when he thought of them, his parents? And now, when the joy of meeting had passed, the horror had come into his mind. He found himself looking at them with strange curiosity. He saw, for the first time, that their bodies were uncouth. Their faces had that ignorant fear in them, the ignorant fear of the animal looking at a strange thing. He was strange to them. Now they were strange to him. And around them, the kitchen and the furniture and the curious silent air and the distant murmuring of the sea was strange. It was not only strange. It was accusing. It was hostile to him. He must be aggressive. He must attack it, them, all of it. Why had he been drawn back? To attack it, them, everything. His body grew rigid and in spite of himself, driven by a strange force, his forehead wrinkled, his eyes narrowed, his mind grew violent and words poured from his lips, almost unknown to him.

'Who would raise a hand to me?' he cried arrogantly. 'And why all this nonsense? I'll tell you why I was expelled. Do you think I committed some crime? Eh? You are ashamed of me. That's the truth. I was expelled because I don't believe in God and I refuse to be a hypocrite.'

The two of them uttered a cry and they looked at him. Now their faces were no longer ignorant with fear. Now everything had been made manifest to them. They knew why he was an outcast, why he was different to them. The bond between them had been broken. But still, a different sort of fear possessed them now. They were afraid of him, not as their son who had become strange to them, but as a dominant strange force that threatened them. But they hid that fear. They looked at one another sadly. Then the mother said irrelevantly:

'Have a cup of tea, my treasure. I'm sure you're longing for one after your voyage.'

'Thanks, mother,' said Peter.

Again there was a period of embarrassment while they had tea. It had become a sad home-coming. They talked casually until bedtime, about the neighbours and all the local happenings. They even laughed together. But they only laughed with their lips. When Peter went to bed his mother came into his room as of old. She tucked him in, uttering blessings and prayers tenderly. Then suddenly she burst into tears, threw her arms around him, and they kissed and wept together, hugging one another fiercely, devouring one another with kisses, shedding salt tears; as if making a savage effort to bridge this unexplainable gulf between them by the force of their natural love.

The next day was Sunday. Peter got up while his father was out milking the cow. In the morning Peter was very gay. One of his old fits of gaiety had possessed him. He pranced about the floor and made his mother waltz with him. He sang songs. He brought a chair out into the yard, put a basin of water on the chair, stripped to the waist and washed there. He shouted merrily to the village people that passed. It was a beautiful Spring morning. Larks were rising as thickly as butterflies, singing their wild triumphant melodies. The whole world was gay. The mother was thrilled with delight and for the moment, that old strange fear was smothered within her. For a moment she imagined that this gay boy was her little son who had come back again to her. Village people, seeing Peter had come back, crowded into the kitchen, welcoming him joyously, while he was having breakfast. They were all dressed in their best clothes, smelling of rough soap, ready to tramp to the parish church at Carra for Mass. The father returned with the milk. Seeing his son's gaiety and the presence of the villagers and the joy that had come upon everybody with his son's return, he also felt exalted.

'He has come back to the land,' he thought, 'now everything will be the same as in my father's time. A son will follow me.'

Peter finished breakfast. He rose from the table, struck himself a violent blow on the chest and then laughed loudly like a peasant.

'Oh!' he said. 'It's great to be back again among my own people.'

'Well said, Peter,' cried several.

Then suddenly an old woman, who sat on the floor on her haunches, put her apron to her eyes, rocked herself and sobbed.

'Oh! indeed, indeed,' she moaned, 'well may you say it, Peter. The roots of the people are as deep as the roots of the earth. We are all of the same kindred and we all share our sorrows. And is it not a sorrow that you had to go wandering in far places after your good mother and your honest father had spent a deal of money to make you a priest? But now that you are back we welcome you, and may you till the earth as well as your father did.'

'He will,' said the people seriously. 'He will.'

Peter smiled, looking at them curiously. He stood in the middle of the floor and they sat around the walls, strange, beautiful faces, all sombre and dignified; mysterious faces of people who live by the sea away from civilization; age-old people, inarticulate, pitiless yet as gentle as children.

Then his mother spoke curtly.

'Indeed he will not till the earth,' she said bitterly. 'Do ye think my son is fit for nothing better than to be a slave to the land like his father? I wanted to make him a clerk first, but he wanted other things.

But now as . . . this other thing is not . . . God's will be done . . . there's many a big house in the town would be glad to get him as a clerk.'

'What's this, woman?' cried Red Michael angrily.

'Don't worry, father,' cried Peter gaily. 'I'll neither be a clerk nor till the earth. I'm an artist now.'

'What?' cried the mother.

The other gaped. Peter laughed again. A roguish gleam came into his eyes. He rushed to his trunk which still remained by the dresser. He brusquely removed two young men who were sitting on it. He raised the lid. 'See, see,' he cried excitedly, as he tossed books on to the floor. 'Look, look.' There was a score of beautiful books and he fluttered the pages of some, showing marvellous pictures to their gaping eyes. Then he brought out paints, brushes, canvas, drawings and all the materials of a painter. Lastly he brought out a portfolio and opened it feverishly.

'These are my own,' he cried with blazing eyes, showing them drawings, one after the other rapidly. 'Take that. Look at that.'

Instead of being enthused, they were horrified. There were drawings in the nude and sketches of fierce, terrible men, everything done with a tremendous, almost uncouth power, the work of a raw, turbulent, half-developed genius; but to them they were visions of the devil incarnate. Without a word they drifted out of the house. Peter took no notice of them. He merely laughed and tumbled the art books and materials back again into the trunk. The gaiety born of his 'creative mania' made him impervious to everything.

'So that's what ye're at,' whispered a voice, that was dry and almost inaudible with horror.

Peter turned around. It was his father who spoke. He saw his father looking at him, with the cunning ferocity and hatred of a wild animal. Still Peter did not flinch. They stared at one another for a few moments. Then the father took his hat and walked out of the house, on his way to Mass.

'Peter,' whispered his mother weakly, 'are you coming to Mass?'

Peter went up to her and kissed her tenderly.

'Next Sunday I'll go, mother,' he said. 'Next Sunday.'

Then she too took her shawl and went out sadly. Left alone in the kitchen, Peter stood motionless for a minute, his eyes blazing, his lips open. Then he cried:

'Yes. I knew I must come back. That scene. The red petticoats. All around the walls. The faces. My God! What faces! What power! At once, before I lose the impression.'

He locked himself in his room and worked all day, sketching the picture of the scene in the kitchen.

That evening all the married children arrived. As relations between them and their parents had been broken for the year previous they came uninvited and obviously determined to cause trouble. Margaret especially was eager to be offensive. A large woman, with a coarse face and avaricious eyes, she flopped on to a chair without removing her enormous red hat. Michael was equally offensive, a large man like his sister, with heavy black eyebrows and little eyes peering from under them furtively, his father's eyes. Joseph, the carpenter, was more subtle, but as hostile as the rest. He had made a good match and he was now very prosperous. He had married a fat middle-aged woman, who had saved a considerable sum of money and he had his hand in all sorts of undertakings. He was silent, astute, and a polite man.

The three of them appeared at the same time. Peter was still in his room with the door locked. He was called out by his mother. He appeared laughing, and taking no notice of the hostile glances directed at him, he shook hands with them all, laughing boisterously.

'Well,' he cried, 'it's nice of you to welcome me home.'

There was silence. The three of them looked at one another. Then Margaret spoke.

'Since we,' she cried haughtily, 'paid for you at college, we'd like to know when you intend to pay us back. When are you going to work, or are you going to make a disgrace of us again with your jig acting?'

'What do you mean?' said Peter flushing angrily.

'Don't speak like that to me,' cried Margaret brutally. 'I heard of what you showed the people this morning. Is it true or isn't it that you have naked women in yer trunk like French postcards – coming back here with yer London smut? What were ye doin' in London I'd like to know. Why didn't ye go to Mass to-day? An' why did ye come back here after bringin' shame an' disgrace on us?'

She would have said much more but Peter's face became so terrible that she stopped, afraid in spite of her arrogance. They all watched him terrified. Then he controlled himself and spoke in a calm voice.

'I forgive you, Margaret,' he said, 'you don't understand. I'm ambitious, just as you are avaricious and mean, just as the rest of you, so I can't blame you for being like myself, only on a lower plane.'

'We don't want to listen to your big talk,' snapped Margaret, encouraged once more by his gentleness.

'Shut up,' he cried, at last losing control of himself. 'I'll tell you what I'm going to do. You'll get your money back, you, all of you, thousands instead of the miserable pounds you paid to educate me. I don't want money. You can have it. All of it. All.'

'Where is it?' said Margaret.

'Here,' he cried tapping his forehead.

They glanced curiously at one another, thinking him insane. Red Michael gaped. The mother wiped her eyes with her apron.

'Yes, it's here,' he continued, tapping his forehead again. 'I only want time. In five years, father, I'll make your name famous all over the world. I'll make thousands, thousands. Only give me time. Work? I'll work the skin off my back. Listen. I've been working for a year in London. I worked as a labourer, as a waiter, as a porter, I can't remember all I worked at, just to get bread and money to pay for lessons and books, to learn my art. That's why I left college, because I wanted to become an artist. Brother Shwartz there, he was a painter. He did something and became a monk. He taught me. He was teaching me for three years on the sly. He taught me to draw, gave me books. He went away. Got fed up and went back to Berlin. Then I told the old president I didn't believe in God and they expelled me. I wanted to become an artist. And look here. Just leave me alone. I want to stay here for a few months and work. A painter in London who liked my work told me to come back and express the . . . you wouldn't understand that. But just you leave me alone and you'll get your money. I don't want money. You can have it. Just let me alone.'

He made a gesture with his hands and dashed back to his room, locking the door after him. The mother burst into tears. Margaret got to her feet.

'Come on, brothers,' she said, 'there's a curse on this house.'

They all left. But Joseph came back again and gave his mother a five-pound note.

'There may be something in what he says,' he muttered. 'It would be best to leave him alone and get him anything he needs. Who knows?'

'God reward you, son,' said the mother, 'I hadn't a grain of flour in the house.'

After that Peter was left alone. But things became lively in the district. Peter cast aside his London clothes and dressed like a fisherman, in raw hide shoes, blue frieze trousers, multi-coloured, woven belt, blue woollen smock and a flat, black, soft felt hat. Between periods of ferocious creative energy he went out fishing and roamed around the district, carousing wildly with the young men and, it was rumoured, making love to the young women. A spirit of turbulent unrest entered the district after his arrival. At first the people loved him for his gaiety, his wildness, and for the fact that he, an educated man, was so familiar with them. But gradually they began to fear him. At first it was the old people who feared him. Then the young people began to fear him. Especially as he was in the habit of drawing sketches of them at the most unusual times, perhaps in the middle of a drinking bout. At home his parents grew more and more hostile, until finally they kept pestering him to leave the place.

However, for six months nobody took any definite action against him. Even the parish priest did not denounce him from the altar, although, indeed, he was very active going round among the people inciting them against Peter.

Then at last the hatred of the people burst forth violently owing to a scandalous orgy that was perpetrated in the village, 'in broad daylight, under their very noses.'

A very old man died. For many years he had been a butt for the gross humour of the young men of the village. They gathered in his cabin every evening, playing cards, telling stories and insulting the decrepit old man in a disgusting fashion. The old man had one son, who, instead of defending his father, took a leading part in this scandalous conduct. Thus, when the old man died, nobody came to the wake but the band of young men, who had formed a sort of rowdy club since Peter's return. An old woman was at first brought in to wash the body and lay it on a deal table in the kitchen. When that was done she went away and no other woman came to participate in the wake. Then a debauch started.

A young man from a neighbouring village, who had recently returned from America, bought two barrels of porter for the debauch. The old man's son made a sort of bargain with the fellow, promising to repay him with the price of his two young pigs, which he guaranteed to sell the following week. Eight of them, including Peter, began to drink the porter.

The debauch lasted for two days. In the meantime a botch carpenter had been brought from Lisheen to make the coffin; but on the second day, at noon, when the coffin was completed, the fellows made the carpenter blind drunk and put him lying in the coffin in the middle of the kitchen floor. The sight was so ludicrous that they were all carried away into an ecstasy of drunkenness. Within an hour they were all lying stupefied on the floor; paralysed with drink. It was a dreadful scene. The village children gathered around the door and some women crept up, talking excitedly and saying that something should be done. It was about four o'clock in the afternoon.

Then Peter was seen coming along hurriedly from his house with a satchel under his arm. They all looked at him in amazement, because they thought he was in the cabin with the others. But a small boy whispered that he had seen somebody steal out by the back door a short time ago. And it was also very strange that after two days' carousing Peter looked quite sober.

With amazement they watched him take a stool in the doorway and begin to sketch the horrible scene within, the corpse, the carpenter lying drunk in the coffin, the stupefied men lying on the floor in gruesome attitudes, the dark kitchen, with sagging, black earthen roof and the silence of death.

They watched him for almost an hour in silence. They were too amazed to speak or to interfere. He worked feverishly, muttering as he worked. The crowd grew rapidly until at last it seemed the whole village had collected, all peering over one another's shoulders to catch a glimpse of the drawing. Even his mother came, but she did not stay. She burst into tears and returned, running to her house, waving her hands.

Then at last he ceased working and jumped up. He put the drawings, he had made several, into his sketch book and cried to the crowd: 'Make way there.' They fell back and he rushed through them.

No one spoke. No one stopped him until he had got clear away.

But then they began to murmur savagely. Then they burst into a frenzied passion suddenly. 'Sacrilege, sacrilege,' they cried. 'Stone him,' others cried. 'Out with him. Kill him.'

They set off towards Red Michael's house at a rush, picking up stones as they went and yelling wildly.

In the meantime Peter had arrived home. The old couple were quarrelling loudly when he entered. When they saw him they both turned on him. There was horror in their faces.

'Get out of my house,' cried the old man.

'Don't worry, father,' said Peter calmly, 'I'm going. I've got a masterpiece. Look.'

He opened the satchel and took out the drawings he had done. They looked and then they both gasped with horror.

'Lord God have mercy upon us,' they cried together.

Then Peter, realizing their horror, was himself stricken with fear. He closed the satchel hurriedly and threw himself at his mother's feet.

'Mother, mother,' he whispered, 'don't look at me like that. Speak kindly to me, mother. Mother, I love you. Forgive me.'

271

'Oh! My darling, my darling,' she wailed, 'there is a curse on you and on me that brought you forth.'

'Begone, begone,' shrieked the old man, 'before God strikes us all dead. Listen. Whisht. Great God!'

It was the people whom he heard coming. Peter jumped to his feet. He saw the maddened people. Then he rushed at the door and bolted it. Almost immediately a shower of stones struck the house. They burst through the windows and pattered on the slates of the roof, while above the sound of their crashing the yells of the people could be heard, drawing closer and urging one another on. The family threw themselves on the floor. The mother began to pray aloud.

That lasted for a quarter of an hour. The people were already battering down the door when suddenly a strange silence fell over them. Then loud whispers were heard: 'It's the priest. The priest has come.' They all fled in confusion. Red Michael timorously opened the door. He saw the priest driving away the last of the people with a big stick. He rushed up to the priest, fell on his knees and embraced the priest's legs. The priest looked at him angrily.

'Get up,' he cried, 'your son has brought a curse on my parish. I give him till night to leave here, NEVER to come back.'

Then he added in a sad voice: 'And may God forgive you, Red Michael, for being his father.'

And so it happened. Within an hour Red Michael had straddled his pony. Peter's trunk was hoisted up and tied with ropes. Father and son set out to the village of Lisheen, six miles away over the mountains, where Peter could catch the night mail cart to the county town. The mother fainted when Peter had left, even though she embraced him coldly when he kissed her goodbye.

Then after lying an hour on the floor where she had fallen she recovered consciousness. Not a soul had come in to succour her. There was dead silence in the village. Dusk was approaching. The murmur of the sea was distinct. She looked about her at the wrecked windows, at the battered door, at the stones that were still on the floor. She shuddered and she rose to her feet. She staggered wearily. Her eyes seemed to be covered with a mist. She rubbed them, but still the mist remained, like a gauze, making everything blurred. Then, suddenly, the gauze cracked. Her eyes opened wide, and everything became distinct. The whole load of her sorrow fell on her mind in a flash. She rushed to the door and looked out along the mountain road by which he had gone. No one, not a speck. Nothing.

Dusk was falling. Night was falling like a shroud

of peace over the heated earth, to pour fresh sap and vigour into the powers of nature, refreshing dew and sleep. But for her there was no night. For ever and for ever she would long in vain for the little one whose naked baby toes she had fondled, to whom she crooned, whose wondering eyes had looked into hers, with the first wondering infant love for the mother at whose breast it fed. For ever and for ever, even through eternity, where damned souls cry out in anguish, he would be lost to her. Lost for ever.

Throwing back her head and raising aloft her hands, she shrieked :

'My curse! My curse on . . .'

Suddenly she dropped her hands. Tears flowed from her eyes and her lips moved in prayer.

WHEN Feeney the fisherman was drowned at sea, Red Barbara, his widow, married a weaver. The weaver came from a distant village, and he had no relatives in our district. It was considered a disgrace that Feeney's widow should marry a weaver who had no relatives. The people also grumbled, saying there would be a smell of urine henceforth in the village, as weavers use it for their looms.

The weaver's name was Joseph. When he arrived he was a young man of thirty. He was strong, well built, with a comely countenance. He had arms like Red Stephen, the blacksmith. His fair hair curled in a straight line over his forehead. He wore black boots, trousers with braces, and a large necktie with white spots in it. He brought his goods on a cart; his loom and a black wooden trunk with a curved top. The women of the village spoke well of him. It was said by the women that Red Barbara would prosper and have many children.

Joseph was much more civilized than the people of our village. He had lived in a town. He could read and write. He had money in his black trunk. He fried bacon for himself and his wife on Sunday mornings. Soon the people of the village came out of their houses on Sundays before going to Mass in

275

order to smell the bacon; with envy in their nostrils. Life became quite different in the village.

Feeney the fisherman had been a careless drunken man. And his wife, although a beautiful woman, was no better than her husband. Their cottage was dirty, badly thatched, with a rocky yard about it and a bedraggled stone fence. But Joseph immediately hired a stonemason and workmen to rebuild the place. After six months it was quite new and beautiful to behold; a little palace in the centre of the ugly village; a white place on an eminence, with a white-washed wall of stone and mortar about it. In our district earth is as precious as gold, since we live on barren, rocky land. But Joseph hired labourers with carts to gather the sweepings off the roads and to dig the rich loam from the common marsh below the village. All this was brought to his house with sand from the seashore. With it he made many little gardens about his house where hitherto there had been rock. He made four gardens in all, three behind the house and one in front. And, lo! The front garden was laid out in flower-beds, with walks of coloured sea pebbles, like gems, between them; and coping stones of brown granite that glistened in the sun. The people marvelled at his wealth, his industry and his strange genius.

Soon flowers grew there; strange flowers which no

276

one in the village had ever seen, golden daffodils and smiling pansies. Joseph became a great man in the village. No man contradicted him when he spoke.

People came from all parts into the village with thread to be woven into frieze cloth. And the people learned that Joseph's weaving room was not an evil-smelling place but a source of wonder and delight. He built a sunken room athwart the end of the house, opening off the kitchen. There he set up the loom and worked at his trade. The people crowded into the kitchen to watch him work and hear him talk eloquently in a soft voice of strange places and strange ideas that came into his sombre mind; ideas about the world, about the elements, about God, about animals, birds and fishes; ideas which had never before been heard in the village. His kitchen became a school. And it was wonderful to see the good cloth grow in the loom, like a miracle.

Other men in Joseph's position might have become arrogant and boastful. But Joseph was a modest man, just and kind in his actions and even sombre in his demeanour; like a man of genius. He often read old books that he kept on a wooden shelf.

At the village well in the evenings, when women drew water and chatted, sitting on their heels, Red Barbara became a person of great consequence. They said to her: 'It was not in an idle hour that God made

your body comely, for you aroused desire in a great
and handsome lover.' She bowed her head and
flushed when they spoke of her thus, knowing that
they expected her to be big with child.

Like a strong beast of the wild forest, that is
trapped and housed in a cage, and fed in unaccus-
tomed idleness, the beautiful creature was dumb-
founded by her new mate and by the luxury that he
had brought into her house. Most of all, she was
terrified by the strange manner in which he loved her.
For she was truly a daughter of our people, primitive
in mind and habits, yet with the grace and beauty
of a queen among women.

She had a small head, like a snake, but with no
malice or subtlety in her large, sleepy, blue eyes.
She had long, golden eyelashes and pretty little teeth
like a young girl. Her hair was red-gold. Her limbs
were long and supple. She walked with a long raking
stride, almost sideways, for her slim body swayed
voluptuously, like a young tree swaying in the wind.
And when she rested she appeared half asleep, without thought; as if she knew she was only made for
love and must always wait for and suffer admiration
or caresses. Her lips were always half open, her
lashes drooped and her little ears, peeping from
beneath her red-gold hair, seemed to be perpetually
listening for words of admiration.

Yet Joseph terrified her, and after a year she had not yet conceived of him. With Feeney it had been different. They had only been married nine months but on the night she heard of his death she suffered a miscarriage and gave birth to twins. They were dead. He had treated her sometimes with cruelty, but she understood him and was happy as his wife. When he threw her down with violence and embraced her she was content. At other times he fondled her like a child. Often he was drunk and beat her. She used to wait patiently for him in the town, standing in the road outside a tavern, while he got drunk with the neighbours. That was not pleasant, but it was the custom among the people. And she was proud of his rough strength and of his bravery at sea when she saw him approaching the rock-bound shore in his boat, riding the foam-embroidered sea, with his black chest bare and dripping with brine.

With Feeney she used to utter little screams of joy and laughed with clenched teeth when he approached her in the darkness of night.

Now, with Joseph, a terrible and sombre quiet had fallen on the house, as when the shining priest mumbles on the altar and phantom angels hover invisibly about the incensed church. Indeed, her new house was like a church, spotless, with rich food and strange instruments and flowers about it. And Joseph was like a priest, an educated man who read books and spoke to the people with authority. Although he was more handsome than Feeney and his skin as fair as a lily, she lay under him in terror, supine and trembling, while he murmured soft words to her that sounded like prayers. He touched her gently and showered gifts on her and gave her a mirror to see herself.

Soon her fear turned into hatred, and when he approached her at night she called out in her mind to Feeney to come and drive his boat-hook through this priestly lecher. And she did not conceive of him.

Joseph began to get worried. A year had passed and there was still no sign of the fulfilment of his happiness. He had made this place beautiful and secured for wife a jewel of womanhood in order that his seed might grow in beauty and happiness. At night he told people how life might be improved and how a new race of men could be produced by making the world beautiful. And lo! He whose fair hair curled in a straight line on his forehead like a ram, had no issue. The people began to whisper among themselves, seeing that Red Barbara was still as slim as a filly. They said: 'He has arms like Red Stephen the blacksmith, but his loins are barren. For she conceived of Feeney the fisherman.' Joseph heard these whispers. He became ashamed and angry. For in our district to be without children is the greatest shame that can come to a man.

However, another year passed before any change was noticed in his behaviour towards his wife or in his sombre calm demeanour. His trade prospered, and his home was now so beautiful that visitors came from afar to look at it on Sundays. And while he was busy perfecting his house and gardens his mind was relieved from contemplation of the fear that had become fixed in his mind. But after two years there was no more to be done. The home was prepared for children and there were none. Then the fear in his mind became active and rebellious. It grew into a red spot and became menacing. His forehead filled with furrows. He became angry at his work and cursed the loom. He threw stones at hens that trespassed in his flower garden. His eyes pursued his wife wherever she went. And when she sat at night near the fire, with her little snake-like, beautiful head motionless, he talked furiously to the assembled neighbours, while the loom rattled and the threads crossed and crossed in frenzied movements. He talked of the world now with outrageous anger and spoke of a purifying spirit that would come to redeem mankind. But the people no longer respected his authority, nor his wisdom, nor his wealth; for his

loins were barren. Among themselves they jibed at
him and at his house and flower garden. For all that
had lost its novelty, and now it seemed that they
had always been there—the wise Joseph and his
flowers and his strange ideas. Lustful young men,
whose blood sang at the sight of Red Barbara, said
with coarse laughter that it was a pity to have her
lying in such a bed.

Then one night Joseph was stricken with a frenzy.
He seized his wife, shook her, and cried: 'How is
this, woman? Am I to die childless?' For a few
moments she looked at him in amazement. Then
she said: 'Feeney would not have died childless.'
Then he struck his forehead like a madman and
cursed wildly. She became afraid and lay still, receiving his violent attentions without a word or
movement. That lasted for many months without
result. A strange look came into his eyes. She became morose and her lips closed over her little white
teeth. Then Joseph consulted an old midwife who
was wise in ancient cures with herbs and sea-craft. She
advised him to put Barbara sitting by the Mermaid's
Cave, on the cliff-shore beyond the village, during
the height of the Spring tide. He did so and Barbara
obeyed, for she feared the strange look in his eyes.

So in the third summer of their marriage she sat
each day by the sea, on a round, smooth rock under

the towering cliffs beside the dark pool, where the mermaids are said to live and may be heard singing on stormy nights to entice the drowning seafarers to their cave. There the sea air is so strong that it enters the blood with the force of an intoxicating drug. The muscles become stiff. The mind swoons and amorous desires come to life in myriads, born of the vigour of nature. The majesty of the towering dark cliffs and the vast bosom of the smiling soft sea are so potent that even tottering old men are drawn thither by instinct from our village when they see the ghost of death approaching. There they are possessed again by a mirage of strength. They walk naked on the scorched rocks. They are seized with a frenzy and try to lift huge boulders with their wrinkled hands. Then they die in peace.

She grew fat. Joseph rejoiced. That Autumn they said she was big with child. Joseph sang at his work. But as Winter came she grew slim once more. The people laughed. Then Joseph lost his senses one day with rage. He locked the door, took a rod and beat her with it. This time she did not bear with him. She struck him with the tongs on the head and knocked him unconscious. The police came and there was trouble. The parish priest had to come and settle the dispute. Joseph fell ill and was confined to his house all Winter.

Next Spring the people saw him moving about his flower garden, pale and haggard, with twitching forehead and a furtive look in his eyes. Nobody came into the house at night since the quarrel; as it was not considered good taste to visit a house where there was discord. But Red Barbara went abroad speaking solicitously of her husband. And she was continually calling to him in the hearing of the people, telling him to beware of the hot sun and not to walk too far along the cliffs in his weak condition. It seemed that she had somehow asserted mastery over him. Sometimes she showed her little white teeth in a smile when she passed the young men of the village.

Joseph continued to do his work of weaving cloth. While he worked there alone in his house he talked to himself and his wife sat motionless by the hearth knitting. At night he lay awake in bed watching her. He would put out his trembling hand and touch her beautiful head as it lay beside him, motionless in sleep, covered with red-gold hair.

As Summer passed his appearance became more wild and disordered. He ceased speaking to the neighbours. When they passed him he glared at them. Barbara accepted the thread from the customers, gave them their cloth and collected the money. She was now mistress of the household. Joseph no longer had any interest in those things.

284

He had begun to live among his flowers and among the birds of the air. He spoke to the flowers and bent down and kissed their petals and called them his children. He also brought food with him to the cliffs and scattered it about him; so that the wild sea birds came hovering about his head. Their cries excited him. He stretched out his hands and sang strange rhapsodies of unintelligible words.

That Winter there was snow and frost. Hordes of birds came about the houses begging for food. Joseph took the door off a little outhouse he had built. On the floor he scattered food for the birds and sat there all day, heavily clothed, talking to the birds, inviting them to come in to him. Soon they became tame. They crowded into the little house – birds of many species – starlings, thrushes, blackbirds, robins, sparrows and tiny wrens. Joseph was very happy among them. He lived all day in the outhouse and worked at his loom far into the night. His cheeks became hollow.

But when Spring came the birds flew away to mate. Joseph was alone again. At dawn he heard them sing; and again at sunset, their soft voices floated on the air. The world was full of song. The sun became warm at noon. His enfeebled body became infused with the delirium of Spring. One day he said to his wife softly at noon :

285

'Lay out my bed on the flagstones on the south side of my house. I am going to lie naked in the sun. I'll grow strong again. Then you will have children by me.'

Barbara looked at him in amazement at first. His eyes were brilliant with sickness and with the wild visions that sick men see. Her eyes became cunning and she thought:

'He has become an old man. Death is upon him.'

She said nothing, but looked at him shrewdly, like a watching bird. Joseph saw the cunning look in her eyes and became angry. He shook his emaciated fist at her and said:

'Ha! You harlot! You expect my doom. But I will arise as strong as a giant from that bed. Lay it quickly before the sun weakens. Quick or the rod will be laid to your back.'

Then Barbara went out into the yard and wept aloud so that the neighbours could hear her. Joseph followed her out shouting and menacing her with his fists. Neighbours gathered hearing the noise. When she saw that the neighbours had come Barbara went indoors, while Joseph began to throw stones at the neighbours and shouted to them to go away and not cast their evil eyes on him.

Then Barbara laid out the bed on the flagstones on the south side of the house. Joseph stripped himself naked and lay on the bed. Barbara went among the neighbours and wept, telling them that Joseph had gone mad and threatened to kill her. They all gathered and watched him lying on his back in the sun.

For a long time he lay still, as if he were dead, with his arms and legs stretched out on the white sheets of the bed, with his cheeks bright red and the ghastly pallor of death on his shrunken body. Then the treacherous Spring sun consumed him with its rays and he began to moan. He rose up, staggered, began to wave his arms, and cried in delirium:

'Where is the witch? She has put a spell on me!'

Then he turned around twice, swooned and fell heavily to the bed. The people rushed up and raised him in their arms. He had a face like a corpse. His lips were white, and a little stream issued from them. They brought him into the house, and the village became silent.

He lived for three weeks, raving at times about a spirit that would come to make the world beautiful and to redeem mankind. He also spoke to little children whom he saw about his bed. Then he died one night when the moon was full and the sea made thunder against the southern cliffs. The whole district followed his corpse to the grave, whispering the many wise things he had said to the people.

Then Barbara lived alone for many months in the little white house on an eminence. Weeds choked the flowers that Summer in Joseph's flower garden. There was no sound from the loom, for she dismantled it and threw it into the outhouse that Joseph had built. When Autumn came the house had begun to look bedraggled, as it was when Feeney the fisherman lived there.

Later three young men came over the sea in a boat from a neighbouring island. They had an accordion with them, and they played it in the boat coming over the sea at sunset. They landed at the rocky shore beyond the village and came to Red Barbara's house. People from the village gathered there also. They toasted her red-gold hair and her beautiful limbs in whiskey they had brought. They caroused for three days, praising her beauty. She took one of them for husband, a young dark fisherman, who had wrists like steel.

Years passed and there were children in Barbara's house. And she was a happy woman of the people once more. Again she stood uttering wild cries, on the mound of boulders above the shore while her husband rode the stormy sea in his boat, fighting with death. Again she led him staggering from the town, singing drunkenly, to her wild bed.

Joseph became a fable in the village.